MAVERICK VALLEY

MAVERICK VALLEY

ROSALIND
AND JON FERRY

Cataloguing information available from Library and Archives Canada.

ISBN 978-1-0698657-0-0 (paperback)
ISBN 978-1-0698657-1-7 (ebook)

Exterior book design: Zizi Iryaspraha Subiyarta
Interior book design: Amit Dey, amitdey2528@gmail.com
Publishing consultant: Geoff Affleck, AuthorPreneur Publishing Inc., authorpreneurbooks.com
Editor: Nina Shoroplova
Photo credit for authors' photo: Susy Carnaghan

To Tom Barrett and Glen Chamberlain
whose adventurous, high-country spirit
is an inspiration to us all.

CONTENTS

CHAPTER 1

THE FALL

It was the kind of mountain ride I'd always dreamed about as a child … through God's country. Ringed by a palette of dainty wildflowers, marmots straddled rocks dating back eons. Moose fed on willows beside the creek, wary of bears and cougars. And venturing into land like this, it paid to be ready for everything that I had feared … and loved.

Up to the left was the dirt trail leading through the sagebrush to Starlight Canyon and the high peaks. Down to the right was Crystal Lake, shimmering in the mid-summer sun. We were almost back at the ranch and looking forward to a long, cold drink — or at least a cold beer cooling in a nearby irrigation ditch.

I was the kid wrangler at the Aspen Ranch, responsible for six young dude riders, four girls and two boys — one of whom, seven-year-old Alex, had never before ridden in terrain like this. Everything seemed kosher … until it wasn't. And my life changed forever.

To this day, I couldn't say exactly what startled Moxy, Alex's supposedly bulletproof horse. But he suddenly exploded and took off at a full run, sweeping past me and my steady lead pony, Faro. Then, 50 yards down the trail, he abruptly stopped, tossing Alex off.

"Get everyone off their horse, and stay calm," I yelled to Janis, the athletic-looking wrangler at the rear of the ride.

Alex wasn't moving when I got to him. He was a limp, unresponsive bundle. His face was grey-white. His head was bleeding. My adrenaline was pounding, but my emergency training kicked in. Alex had no pulse and wasn't breathing. So, I immediately started CPR.

"Janis, call the ranch," I ordered. "We need medics as soon as possible. Tell them it's an emergency and we have an unconscious boy who's had a fall on the trail. Have them bring a stretcher, neck brace, all the usual stuff."

Janis pulled the cellphone from the back pocket of her jeans, summoned help, and made sure the other children dismounted and remained quiet and collected.

Then, the shouting stopped. And there was silence. The only movement appeared to be that of stately Engelmann spruce swaying in the wind.

Out of the corner of my eye, I looked up and saw Alex's nine-year-old brother, Simon, inching warily toward me. He looked ghost-like. "Is Alex okay," he asked. "Is he okay?"

"No, I'm afraid he's had a bad fall," I replied, believing honesty to be the best policy. "Do you know what upset Moxy?"

"No," Simon said. "We were just fooling around. Just having fun. That's all. I never thought he'd take off like that."

I never thought Moxy, a Morgan gelding, would act like that either. But then you never know what horses will do if they're frightened by something and their survival instincts kick in and spur them on. They're prey animals, after all.

What I did know was that this was my worst nightmare, and I would be blamed. The parents of these two children had entrusted me with their children's safety, and now one of them lay lifeless at my feet. There was no walking this back.

Help, though, arrived sooner than I thought it would, in the form of a couple of burly male paramedics. They continued further CPR before lifting Simon's body onto a stretcher and carrying him gingerly down the winding path to the ranch's main lodge.

Janis, looking suitably subdued, went with them. I stayed behind and told the remaining children what was going on … or most of it.

"This was an extremely unfortunate accident, and Alex will get the best care going," I said lifelessly. "So, pray for him and wish him well and do all you can to enjoy the rest of your stay."

We walked all the horses back to the barn, unsaddled them, and put them out to pasture in the field furthest from the lodge. Then, I prepared myself for the most painful inquisition I had ever faced.

Alex's parents, I'd been warned, were wealthy medical people from back East. She was a nurse called Alice, and he a doctor. They told me with tears in their eyes that the paramedics had done all they could to help Alex, but that he'd been pronounced dead at 5:15 p.m.

That was when my heart stopped. I cried, hugged Alice, and said how very sorry I was. She in turn embraced me before asking what exactly had spooked Moxy and caused Alex to be thrown and fall so hard to the ground.

"I wish I knew. I really do. I've never had something like this happen on one of my rides," I said. My lips were trembling. "Moxy is usually such a good, steady horse. That's why I chose him for Alex."

Then, a strange thing occurred. Instead of continuing to press me for further details of the accident and my role in it, Alice talked about her son's existing health condition. She said Alex seemed mostly to be a robust, active boy. But recently he had suffered from recurring headaches, and she had sent him to a physical therapist.

"All the tests came back negative," she continued, as if speaking to a fellow clinician. "But like many young children, Alex has a large head, which makes him susceptible to landing on it. His neck muscles are weak and immature."

I wasn't surprised that Alice would refer to her son in the present tense, as if he were still alive. But I was a bit taken aback that she would raise the issue of his recurring headaches at this time. And, after paying my respects, I left her to comfort the shell-shocked Simon.

But, yes, I had sensed Alex had a bigger hat size than was normal for a child of his age. It was something, though, I hadn't thought any more about … until that awful day. And I didn't believe I would have done anything differently if I had.

I loved horses, and had been riding since I was five. I had seen a lot during that time of what can go wrong in the blink of an eye — and how alert one must be around these large, flighty animals. There is no right way, moreover, to come to terms with the death of a horse rider in your care, especially if it's a child.

What I can say is that, for years, Alex's passing and my struggle to expunge my guilt for what happened left me with a profound feeling of loss and loneliness. Grief sticks to you like a stain after rolling over you like a wave. And I knew from the get-go that a few of the Aspen Ranch guests found it hard to be around me. They gave me a wide berth, feeling no doubt I was somehow cursed.

Others, rocked by grief of some type themselves, were supportive, but treated me with kid gloves. To them, I was a kind of China doll. But never before had I felt I was a fragile victim, even though my family life wasn't anything to write home about.

So, this was a terrible new burden I had to bear as an impressionable, 20-year-old woman. And there seemed to be no obvious way out.

CHAPTER 2

LOVE RUSH

At first, I couldn't figure out why so many people were leaning on the rails of the buck fence overlooking the main pasture. But then it became clear … or at least clearer.

They were ghouls waiting to watch Rory, the ranch's boastful foreman, and Luke, the ranch's youthful Mr. Fix-It, do something really stupid — race each other bareback over the pasture's treacherous set of irrigation ditches. A fall by either horse or either rider could have proved disastrous.

I was still at the barn, having just finished unsaddling a half-dozen dude horses after their afternoon ride. But I had a good view of a bad situation, and my nerves were on edge.

It had been only a month since seven-year-old Alex had fallen to his death off a ranch horse. And already, it seemed, two young men at that ranch were risking their lives — and those of their horses — in a ludicrous and potentially lethal display of testosterone.

Rory, twenty-six, with an ego as large as a house, and Luke, a calm and modest nineteen-year-old, were polar opposites. They loathed each other, largely because both were busy trying to ingratiate themselves with me.

The cheering from the cheap seats had started, and the horses were snorting with excitement. But what was about to take place was less a test of the skill of the two riders or the speed of their mounts and more a mad, neo-medieval jousting tournament.

Rugged Rory was aboard Jasper, a speedy Quarter Horse, and the lean, painfully reserved Luke was riding Comet, an agile Arab-cross.

The leathery Jeff, one of the ranch's older cowboys, stood erect between the two men and acted as the official starter of the race. Holding his right hand high above his head, he turned to look at each of them in turn, saying he wanted to have a "clean, safe race with no monkey business."

"Are you ready?" he asked. And when they both gave him the thumbs up, he counted slowly and deliberately down from ten to one. And then he barked "go … go."

And they were off, kicking up a cloud of dust and scaring the coyotes and other wild critters lurking in the sagebrush. It was all one big blur.

Most of the cabin girls, ranch hands, and other spectators, I suspect, were hoping Rory would fall flat on his face. But that was not to be. Though he started poorly and trailed the smoother Luke for much of the race, Rory spurred Jasper at the last minute so harshly he overtook Comet, who stumbled spectacularly at the last ditch.

Leaping off his horse, Rory bowed to the crowd, yelling: "Who is Number One at the ranch?" And when the inevitable boos followed, he cocked his ear at them and announced, "I can't hear you."

The taciturn Luke, meanwhile, didn't bother going over to Rory to shake his hand. He was more concerned with the state of Comet's legs and whether they needed wrapping.

The loud party was soon over. And the race settled nothing, especially as I was in no mood to congratulate either of the love rivals. But I couldn't help feeling that the older, cockier one won. And cockiness was what I needed most at that time, not someone I had to coax into conversation.

Rory hugged me, and not for the first time. Luke, who was bent over Comet, looked up briefly and shrugged. He wasn't about to do anything to validate what had taken place, at least, not in front of me.

That night, I slept with Rory in my cabin for the first time. He was awash in alcohol, and I had stomach cramps, so it wasn't the most beautiful of experiences. But it got me out of the funk I'd been in ever since Alex's tragic death, which, with all the ensuing publicity, was starting to seem more and more like a prison sentence.

My self-confidence had been shattered by the young boy's death. And having a handsome man with huge self-assurance wanting me and showing off to me seemed to take my pain away.

I got lost in the moment, and Rory's swagger and bravado made me forget myself. He was overwhelmingly affectionate and looked deep into my eyes as if nothing else anywhere was as important. His passion was a turn-on, and I was swept off my feet.

In the meantime, the wheels of the justice system moved slowly in the case of poor Alex, whose life had been taken from him a month earlier, just as he was learning to ride.

Despite the seemingly clear-cut nature of his horse fall, the coroner's office decided to hold an inquest on the grounds that the exact cause of it was "unclear" and there were "public concerns surrounding the circumstances of the child's death."

The press release didn't elaborate on what those circumstances were, but I reckoned I knew them only too well.

My parents, living in Maverick Valley, a hundred miles to the southwest, weren't exactly supportive about my role in Alex's fall … or at least my choice of a summer job.

They said they'd warned me, based on their extensive experience in running a dude ranch, that my signing on as a kid wrangler meant being blamed for anything and everything. And the wealthier the kids' parents, the more unpleasant and vindictive they usually turned out to be.

I was, however, comforted by the attitude of Frank Smithson, the Aspen Ranch's gentlemanly owner. He insisted that, from all he'd heard, I'd done nothing wrong and could continue on as one of his most valuable employees. But he added that, if the inquest found I had violated the rules, it might be a different story. In any case, he suggested I keep my head down.

My way of doing this, of course, was to embark on a full-blown relationship with Rory … which, in hindsight, was not the wisest move, emotionally vulnerable as I then was.

But towering over me were the mountains in all their majesty. And at that point they were saying this too shall pass, and the trail will set you free … if it doesn't kill you first.

Also, I had been raised on a farm in the country, in Maverick Valley, and I think rural people are more used to seeing life and death in all their various desperate, defiant cycles. City people tend to be more cushioned from these things. Someone else runs the snowblower, picks up the trash, fixes the plumbing … or mourns.

Country folk also appear more inured to climate change and other vagaries of nature. And Maverick Valley certainly had its fair share of those, with constant flash floods, forest fires, and waves of extreme heat, cold, and high winds. Perhaps that makes valley residents better equipped to deal with tragedy. They get over it quicker. Or at least that's what I told myself at the time.

CHAPTER 3

HOPE

With its sky-hugging mountains, 360-degree views and raw, restless spirit, the mushrooming town of Homage bordering Maverick Valley is a place of great beauty and high drama. But it remains a little rough around the edges, with the feel of a recently tidied up — or tarted up — mill town.

Over the past 150 years, it's muddled its way through a series of births, rebirths, and reincarnations … or, as long-term Homage residents like to call them, "invasions."

Trappers, fur traders, missionaries, and farmers were followed by miners, loggers, millhands, and hippies and yuppies … and, of course, mountain-bikers and culture vultures. And let's not forget adventure-seeking climbers, hikers, windsurfers, and professional photographers like myself.

Homage had turned into a refuge for those wishing to escape both the bright lights of the big city and the petty squabbles of rural life. It was a town forever on the move … though with many more people moving in than moving out, house prices had been moving inexorably upwards.

That's when some free spirits started cashing in their built-up home equity and heading on up the Homage River … to a valley where cabins were cheap, views jaw-dropping, and property came with acres of elbow room.

Maverick Valley, where I grew up, had for some years attracted the kind of independent-minded person who sought to live in a less stuffy environment with a more expansive lifestyle … albeit one vulnerable to flooding, forest fires, and other manifestations of nature's wrath.

The offbeat valley was then discovered by dreamers and developers willing to cough up top dollar for land they believed would yield a bonanza similar to that of such billionaire havens as Jackson Hole in Wyoming, and Whistler in British Columbia.

But since maverick-minded independents weren't always the most emotionally intelligent, it remained a spot where the supposedly simple life was anything but simple. And supposedly bold ideas were all too often taken down cul-de-sacs and quietly strangled.

Negative thoughts, though, were the last things on my mind as I headed out from the downtown Homage lawyer's office where I'd signed the possession papers for the Maverick Valley lodge of my dead father and in-care mother.

Despite a teeter-totter of a life, I was finally where I'd always intended to be … a year or so from the Big 40 and in charge of my own destiny.

The 25-minute journey to my newly acquired lodge took me along a gloomy two-lane road through a dense rainforest that suddenly opened up to provide a stunning view of the Homage River in a blaze of sunlight.

There, towering thousands of feet above was a vision of heaven … the Phantom Mountains, with their jagged summits rising from massive alpine glaciers. They signalled that, after nearly two decades of domestic strife, career struggle, and a single mom's life, I was home at last.

A sense of relief enveloped me as I slowed my pickup to a halt and conjured up an image of a pasture-based retreat for horses, dogs, and other animals … with room for everyone from weekend warriors to artists, writers, and wedding guests. And let's not forget trick-or-treating children.

But my greatest hope was that my riverside home would prove an anchor for my restless 18-year-old daughter, Jess, giving her the stability she craved, having suffered with me through my tempestuous marriage, ugly divorce, and one too many household moves.

What was immediately lacking was a metal sign visible from the road, declaring that Shadow Mountain Lodge had re-opened for business … and that I was the proud owner. I needed Sandy, the local blacksmith, a long-time maverick, to serve up one of his signature pieces.

But the first thing I did on exiting my truck was not to enter the front door of the timeworn farmhouse. Instead, I took a circuitous route down a pebbled path to the Homage River, knowing for better or for worse I was wedded to it now.

A swirling, foaming, mercurial watercourse, the river poured down from towering icefields to the Pacific Ocean, nourished along the way by several large, glacier-swollen, sediment-bearing tributaries.

It teemed with salmon and trout, with an estuary providing habitat for bald eagles, hummingbirds, great blue herons, turkey vultures and grizzlies, black bears, black-tailed deer, coyotes, cougars, and elk.

Truly a river of golden dreams, it flowed methodically and rhythmically, while asking little more of stressed humanity than grudging recognition and respect. It was how I wanted to live my life from now on — without shame or lame insecurity.

I was prepared to work hard, as I always had done. But I wanted to be like the river and be free — or as free as this love-starved, photogenic property would let me.

I stood at the edge of river, picked up a well-rounded rock, held it with my eyes closed — and squeezed hard. All the trials and tribulations I'd experienced over the years welled up inside me like an overflowing bucket. And I let go of them, breathed out and started to sob.

Then, I tossed the rock as if throwing away a piece of heavy debris … and let the river swallow it up.

CHAPTER 4

CONFIDENCE

Blacksmith Sandy Jetson had been recommended to me by Jack, owner of Central Motors, the main gas station in Homage.

Jack said Sandy was "a bit of a lad," whatever that meant, but was responsible for most of the signs and other metal work in Maverick Valley … or at least most of the interesting stuff.

"The hard thing is trying to get hold of Sandy as he's into so many things these days," he said, grimacing. "He's always branching out."

"That's what a lot of folks in the valley are doing these days," I replied, though not quite sure what kind of "branching out" he was referring to … and whether of the legal or illegal variety.

Jack gave me directions to Sandy's place, saying you had to take the first right past the monastery, then go right up the hill and it was on the left. He didn't exactly seem very positive about my chances of finding it.

"It's heavily forested there," he said. "And I don't think there's a sign indicating when you've arrived. Also, he's kind of a secretive guy and doesn't have a landline."

I knew I had finally arrived at the property when I found myself facing a large, weathered Dutch barn. It was loaded with a dizzying array of electrical wires and cables and tools, machinery and other metal objects, both dated and new.

I was also confronted by a couple of noisy blue heelers, dogs known both for their intelligence and loyalty … and for having an independent streak.

Sandy was inside the barn, fixing a bike for his sporty son, Joel, a competitive racer who, he said, had honed his skills in what was some of the best country for mountain-biking around.

"That's why the pups look so healthy, all that up-and-down and in-and-out keeps them super fit," Sandy told me flirtatiously, as I gingerly patted one of the dogs. "But what can I do for you?"

"I am looking for a sign for my place," I replied, noting that the color of Sandy's eyes matched that of his light blue T-shirt. "It's just up the road by the river, under Shadow Mountain."

"Oh, you mean the Gilbert spread," he said. "I heard about Doctor Dan's death. And Mary isn't in good health either, is she? I'm sorry about that."

"Yes, word travels fast. I'm the long-lost daughter and new owner. I'm calling it Shadow Mountain Lodge and turning it into something that's well-run, visitor-friendly, and looks the part."

"You'll need to send a good, strong message then," he suggested. "Something that announces you've arrived at — or rather returned to — Maverick Valley. Just tell me what you want."

"I'd like a sign that's bold, beautiful, and etched with mountains and eagles," I stated, "something that makes the heart soar … like the monastery."

"Well, the convent's current sign isn't anything to write about," Sandy said. "But we'll see what we can do. I'll drop off a sketch in a couple of days, and you can tinker with it."

The tinkering didn't take long. Sandy brought the weighty metal sign, along with son Joel, who was apparently in one of his rare smiling moods. And Joel and my daughter Jess bolted it to the wooden horizontal bar above the ranch entrance gate. They both seemed as pleased with it as they were with each other … and as I was with Sandy. It all was cozy and copacetic.

I stood back from the sign and thought how it made just the welcoming statement I was looking for. The laser-cut image of an eagle in full flight against a bank of mountains raised the first impression of the lodge to a whole new level.

We celebrated with a beer in the lodge's living room, where I thought to myself this old dump badly needs a refresh. Then, I asked Sandy whether he still shod horses, as I was planning to keep a half-dozen of my own at the ranch.

"So, you're a keen rider? I know your mother was, but she always seemed to have her hands full with other things."

"Yes, it's been a bit of a passion of mine ever since I was a kid," I explained. "It keeps me energized and grounded."

"But speaking to your question, I no longer shoe horses," he said, stroking back his sleek hair. "My body just won't stand it anymore. I miss being around horses, though, and would be happy to go for a ride with you some time."

"Sure, let's do that. I'll let you know when I've found a horse that will go gentle on a banged-up old blacksmith," I joked. I smiled confidently, reminding myself that couples who ride together tend to thrive together.

That night, I had the best sleep in a long time. It was deep and long and free of dark visions. And Jess was up fashionably late as usual. So, we breakfasted together, and for once took the time to have a good chat.

I explained to her this was the new beginning I was waiting for … and that I'd love her input on how we could turn the lodge and accompanying land into an adult-and-kid-friendly retreat of which we both could be proud.

"Okay, Mom," Jess said in her usual non-committal way, untangling her long, dark-brown hair and twisting her fingers slowly through it. "Well, I'm ready," she laughed, while rolling her eyes as if she'd played this game with me before.

I acknowledged that our relationship had been strained of late. And I said I could appreciate her feelings of frustration about the apparent waywardness of our storm-tossed little family. But I added that, with her brains, beauty, and energy, she had a bright future, and I was sure a great tide of opportunities would soon be coming her way.

"Seize them," I commanded in my best mother-teacher mode, handing her a coffee in a red mug. "Make the most of those opportunities. I wasted a few when I was your age, or just a little older, and look how it cost me."

"Oh, Mom, you can't stop moralizing, can you," she replied, adding she had no plans to get pregnant at an early age, as I had done. "What I think is that, after all we've been through, it's time we started to kick back and actually enjoy ourselves."

I agreed with her, knowing that the triple whammy of moving house, her mother's divorce, and the recent loss of a grandparent would be highly stressful for a teenager wrapped up in a maelstrom of swirling feelings.

All of that — and a sea of guilt that refused to subside after nearly two decades — still posed a challenge for me.

CHAPTER 5

HORSING ABOUT

I was doing some shopping in town and looking forward to my afternoon riding date with Sandy when I popped into the laid-back Lazy Loungers for a cup of coffee described as "the finest in the world."

And I rediscovered why I still liked the coastal town of Homage, with its eclectic mixture of urban progressiveness and rural assertiveness — and, of course, its dry sense of humor.

The billboard at the next-door bar, for example, advertised it was selling "beer as cold as your ex's heart." Which certainly resonated with me.

Homage was a place where you could find yourself beside a Trump-supporting logger in a lifted Tacoma truck or a liberal stoner in a Kombi van ... or both at the same time. It was where folks still believed in the irony reflected in the waterfront sign that stated: "Private land. Trespassers welcome."

The problem was that, as well-heeled careerists and cottagers poured in, area house prices started to soar. And the community attracted those who liked to "protect their investment" by fencing off every inch of their land … not to mention telling "strangers" to take a hike.

So much for equity and diversity. These NIMBYs even had issues with free-roaming mustang horses they claimed were drinking too much water, chewing up too much grass, and causing "insufferable" traffic snarl-ups.

The territorial venom became so toxic it got out of hand. And a forest ranger found the bodies of eight wild horses that had been killed and left to rot on public valley land. Investigators believed the animals were hunted down and "deliberately shot." So much for live and let live.

But as poet Ted Hughes noted, nothing in life is free. There's always a debt to be paid. In this case, feral animals paid the price for the intolerance of humans who prided themselves on their love of freedom, only to deny it to other free creatures.

These days, "influencers" promote the idea that you can achieve success in all areas of your life, from romance to religion. But most of us know we can't have it all, and tough choices have to be made.

Mavericks also seem to understand this. Which is why some believe their best option is to head out of town to one of the last livable areas in North America where you can still find independent-minded people who will at least leave you alone.

They also recognize this is a privilege that increasingly comes at a cost. Pretty well everything, up to and including the land itself, will set you back more in marvelous Maverick Valley. It's the price you pay for all that elbow room.

The original maverick, of course, was a free-spirited, 19th-century Texas land baron called Samuel Maverick, who refused to brand his cattle. Yet, most humans cannot stand too much liberty. They elect governments whose mission is to tax, well, everything. And public parks are packed with signs telling you all the things you cannot do … just in case you were wondering.

Even in downtown Homage, though, parking remains free. So are the mountain views. And you can still buy adult books for two dollars apiece or toddler's mittens for far less.

In the more remote parts of adjoining Maverick Valley, your choices may be more limited. But the smiles are wider, the greetings warmer and the views broader. And that makes it far easier to cling to your piece of earthly paradise.

My ride with Sandy went swimmingly. The western horses, two of the three that I had been gifted by a nearby rescue sanctuary, appeared to enjoy the cool of the trail through the forest down by the river. And Sandy, with his lean muscles and longish, sandy-colored hair, was chatty, without being too mouthy or chock-full of opinions.

I especially liked the way he kept his cool when his paint mare Mitzy was spooked by some crows in the trees and took off. He just went with her, and gently but firmly turned her until she stopped.

As a lifelong horsewoman, I'd had my fill of out-of-control horses and riders. And after living through a marriage to a man with a hair-trigger temper, I longed to be free from anger and aggression. I was looking for the calmness that comes with caring … but not caring too much. I wanted a tender hug rather than a suffocating crush.

As we approached the lodge, we rode side by side for a while until Sandy affectionately extended his arm to reach out for mine. We locked our hands together and smiled.

We unsaddled the ponies back at the barn, again with no drama, and strode into the lodge for tea. Then, we went out to the deck, an area I planned to pretty up to give the lodge a focal point for hanging out. The conversation flowed freely, especially when we talked about horses, my favorite subject.

At one point I asked Sandy about his Irish-born father, who was also a blacksmith and farrier, and how it had been for him, as an immigrant, to make a living here in the valley.

"It was tough for him, because of his drinking," he said. "And it's been tough for me, because I was his son and never knew what he would do next. But I've never just done one thing. I've always been a man of many colors. And I certainly never relied on him."

Self-reliance, I've learned, is rarely a bad trait in a man. It certainly beats neediness and dependency. But living in a faraway place with few friends can also lead to a special kind of burnout that comes from isolation, a lack of light, and a shortage of company. In the Far North, they call it cabin fever.

I wondered who exactly kept Sandy sane — apart from his bike-riding son — and what he did all day when he wasn't making metal signs for pushy new lodge owners.

But that was fodder for another date, which now seemed both inevitable, welcome and, given the currently available alternatives, even dreamy. And as poet Langston Hughes famously said, you have to cherish your dreams because, without them, life is cold and barren.

CHAPTER 6

PARADISE

While I moseyed my way up the forested driveway of the Catholic monastery, I had a strong sense of déjà vu, recalling the week I'd spent there at Easter time back when my marriage was falling apart and Jess was in youth camp.

That was a week of peace and quiet, listening, spiritual reflection … and physical toil on the farm that the nuns operated there. It was a life-saver for me, or at least a life-changer.

For one thing, the retreat taught me a valuable lesson about the need to stay focused and not let myself get yanked in a million different directions. Monastic living cuts off the distractions of lay life.

Life at Our Lady of the Rosary convent, though, was far from devoid of emotion. Its statement-making, post-and-beam building came complete with chapel, dining room, community room, library, infirmary, conference room, bedrooms, visiting rooms, and a retail shop to sell monastic products (from artwork to jam, cheese, and hand-made soaps).

Oh, and it faced directly out onto the mountains. The views alone were divine. In fact, the convent seemed very much a stairway to God and the good life … though I had heard that, financially speaking, it was struggling and looking for a more worldly savior.

The quarter-section of land on which the monastery sprawled included an orchard of mature fruit trees. And I remember one day during my week-long stay receiving detailed instructions on tree care from a farmer known locally as Johnny Appleseed, though his real name was Appleton.

Bearded and bedraggled, Appleseed was always smiling … for no obvious reason. And in the afternoon, he brought along with him a non-smiling friend. That friend, I now remember, was my metal-sign blacksmith Sandy, who had apparently been hired then by the sisters as a general handyman.

In those days, of course, Sandy acted and looked more like a regular cowboy. But I later heard a rumor that he and Johnny were involved in some kind of valley marijuana production … unlikely though that may have sounded, given their obvious physical, mental, and social differences.

In the meantime, I spoke to the prioress, Sister Claudette, about ways we could mutually benefit from having guests at my nearby Shadow Mountain Lodge regularly visit her nunnery and its farm.

The sister was enthusiastic about welcoming them to the gift shop and even the chapel. But when it came to the convent's agricultural operations, she became a bit grumpy, stating that it was off-limits for a variety of reasons, including the safety of the visitors.

"I'm sorry, but the sisters have enough work to do there all day," she huffed, "without tourists tramping all over the place, messing things up, and distracting them."

I didn't pursue the subject. But it did cross my mind that, if the nunnery really was hard up for cash, growing pot on its own land might well prove a lucrative option.

Now, some might say the likelihood of nuns making hay — or hard cash — from getting others high might seem a little far-fetched. But I heard that a group of cannabis-growing nuns in California had already done just that. Though not part of an official religion, these "Weed Nuns" reportedly viewed themselves as activists, healers, and business people.

Also, small-scale marijuana cultivation was now legal in Maverick Valley and the area surrounding it. Labor costs would be minimal. The work ethic would be there. And who better to manage things from the outside than green-thumb Appleseed?

When I mentioned this later to Sandy at our downtown Homage dinner date, he just shrugged. "You must be kidding. Appleseed couldn't organize his way out of a paper bag. He's usually off with the fairies."

"But he can grow anything anywhere," I replied energetically. "All he needs is a well-organized partner or businessperson."

I pointed out how I remembered Appleseed and Sandy, years ago, instructing a group of nuns on the finer points of tree-pruning. But Sandy didn't seem to recall me being there. And I let the subject drop, though I did have the distinct feeling that he was, if not a closed book, at least someone who kept his business dealings close to his chest.

Instead, I asked him about his son, Joel, whom I assumed would be one of his favorite topics of conversation. Yet he wasn't to be drawn on that subject either. He simply said the young man was struggling at school and had got in with the wrong crowd.

"I hope Jess can be a good influence on him," he added.

I countered that Jess was also at sixes and sevens, but that she already had a boyfriend, Matt, who was also a competitive mountain biker. The only problem was that he was usually either recovering from injury or away at big biking events. "And wherever Matt goes," I added, "he seems to have groupies hounding him."

"Yes, I guess that's why Joel gets so envious of him," Sandy agreed. "He never stops whining about mighty Matt and his high-and-mighty attitude."

"I don't know anything about that," I replied, quizzically. "But I remember my late teenage years and how little things, yet alone big ones, threw me off course … even here in paradise."

"You call this paradise?" Sandy said. "Paradise Lost maybe. But, believe me, Maverick Valley is no Garden of Eden. And with all the gender-bending going on, I think the relationship between the sexes is worse than ever. That's why so many men stay away from women, and so many women seem so keen to move back into the monasteries."

I said I found it hard to disagree with him. But I didn't feel like getting drawn into a heavy political discussion, sensing our usually bubbly chat was fast going down a proverbial rabbit hole.

What I did I know was that our first kiss would have to wait at least until our next date … if there ever was one.

CHAPTER 7

BIKES, HORSES, AND BUSINESS

Business at the lodge turned out to be better than I had expected. Sure, I'd had to pour money into the place for everything from new fencing to a fancy metal roof. But I found no shortage of families anxious to kick back, relax, and enjoy the lovely acreage with its horses, goats, rabbits, and ostriches.

Or to take part in a more rigorous adventure.

The river-rafting operation next door was constantly in high demand. It was also expensive. And mountain-biking was always popular ... so popular that, with Sandy's approval, I hired Joel part-time as a bike wrangler. His job was to take paying visitors up the mountain trails and make sure they didn't break their necks on the roller-coaster ride down.

Joel, for once, liked his job. He also loved the fact that it gave him a chance to flirt with Jess, who made up for her lack of bike-riding experience with her burgeoning equestrian talent.

As for the lodge horses, I hadn't decided yet whether to rent them out as trail horses or keep them just for use by Jess and me and our friends and relatives to ride.

I knew I didn't want to have to re-live in any way the trauma I felt — and still feel on occasion — for Alex's death on that fatal ranch ride all those years ago. But I thought it might be good to hold regular, equine-assisted learning programs for children — especially those with autism or other disabilities.

However, I realized that I am an "ideas person" who can get ahead of herself and become easily overwhelmed. Sometimes, rather than running off in all directions — and running out of steam — I need to give my head a shake and steady up.

In the meantime, I directed horse-loving guests to a nearby ranch that offered guided outings, using rescue animals. The husband-and-wife wranglers there were pros at what they did. And invariably the dudes returned refreshed and ready for further action after one- or two-hour rides that meandered along forested trails beside the river.

Horses, though, remained my passion. And I had the lodge's dilapidated outdoor arena re-fenced and re-sanded for Jess's and my personal use.

Jess then made a big effort to interest Joel in learning to improve his riding skills … and perhaps to become a bona fide wrangler. But she said he was far too impatient with Chester, the supposedly steady sorrel she had picked out for him.

She reminded me how I had once told her that one of the greatest hindrances to good horse-riding was rushing things. And I had quoted Tom McGuane, the Montana writer and team roper who said asking a horse to absorb more than it is capable of causes it anxiety, which severely sets back its training.

Jess felt that Joel was not only impatient, but sometimes downright abusive to the gelding, manhandling him angrily and smacking him on the head and neck. And that was a complete turn-off for her.

Her elusive boyfriend, Matt, on the other hand, was gentler with his hands and more willing to learn and listen … at least whenever she could persuade him to visit.

The main issue now for me, though, was to find a level-headed person who would be willing to help manage the place, preferably someone who knew a thing or two about animals.

So, just for the summer, I hired Chelsea, a pint-sized, upbeat, British-born woman who was finishing up her vet studies. Everybody seemed to like both her knowledge of animals and her apparently boundless energy. In fact, she seemed to be exactly the kind of comrade-in-arms Jess and I needed at this key juncture.

The second pressing issue was one that could have far greater, long-term consequences. A major city-based development firm, Peregrine Holdings, which boasted of substantial political clout, had applied to build a resort of its own just down the road from mine. And it stood to dwarf my humble operation in every way.

One of its smiley senior executives, Martin Sterling, had even taken me out to lunch at the RideOut, the mountain-bike-friendly cafe in Homage, to pick my brains and garner my support.

In his big-city civvies, Martin stuck out there like a sore thumb. But he more than made up with it by being tall and exceptionally good-looking … only to rub me up the wrong way by butchering our chat with banal business jargon.

Would I be interested in investing in this "exciting new opportunity" or perhaps even "divesting" myself of my "somewhat dated operation" and selling it to his "forward-thinking" corporation? "We really want to create something big here, something that moves the needle," he said.

"Well, no, I wouldn't," I replied firmly. "I'm not interested either in selling Shadow Mountain Lodge or investing in a development I don't believe in. Like many others in the valley, I prefer small to big … and my needle is not for moving."

Martin insisted, however, that his company had rock-solid county and state support from politicians determined to expand tourism — and create jobs — in the so-called Sky-to-Sea Corridor.

I suspected, of course, that was a lie … because several Maverick Valley residents had already voiced their fierce opposition to the yet-to-be-built "garish-looking, outsized resort." They claimed in a media release that it would "destroy the whole spirit of our farm-friendly mountain valley whose beauty is unsurpassed in this part of the world."

There were, though, other locals who strongly supported the project, posting that it would "save our valley from poverty and irrelevance." And, though more anonymous, they were equally vociferous.

Later that afternoon, I discussed the matter with Sandy, who said he understood why I might not like the idea of competition moving in. But there was no stopping progress.

"You either grow into something or you slow to nothing," he said in his usual clipped way. "More visitors mean more customers, and more customers mean more services. We are no longer a remote, lonely, underserved valley."

I told him I couldn't disagree more. In fact, I said I was now thinking of running for council on a save-the-valley platform … and I knew I could win. A bad marriage had taught me that, as the saying goes, if you don't stand for something, you will fall for anything.

Sandy slunk off in a huff, saying I should stop being such a NIMBY. "Think of Jess or Joel, do you simply want young people like them to have to leave? I mean, where are all the good jobs around here? They're nowhere."

Jess, of course, heard us arguing and tried to intervene. She said she was tired of angry couples. "Can't two people just get along for once?" It was a good question, and one I had been asking myself for some time … if not my entire life.

Opposites, some say, attract. And you do hear of couples who manage to get along despite having very different outlooks and political views. Actress Mila Kunis, for example, has managed to stay married to Ashton Kutcher for a decade — even though she claims she's a confirmed pessimist, while he, like me, is a die-hard optimist.

However, I was starting to realize that I needed a partner who, if not totally in sync with me in all ways or on all levels, at least shared my core values … and sense of what was right.

CHAPTER 8

KOOKIE CABBIE

Having lived in rural or small-town places in the Pacific Northwest most of my life, I've observed at least a couple of things. One is that places off the beaten track tend to attract eccentrics and other offbeat people who yearn to start a new life … or escape from an old one. The other is that eccentrics often seem to hold strong, fixed opinions and unshakeable beliefs that appear to contradict each other.

Look no further than Maverick Valley resident Dale Carrick, the area's most talkative — and most talked about — cab driver. Dale was a lanky, bearded, divorced man in his fifties, who appeared as addicted to health and environmental causes as he was to unhealthy recreational drugs. He had bad body odor and his cab reeked of skunk.

He said he hated violence, but voiced his support for acts of violent sabotage that, in the past five years, had twice cut the main cable of Homage's much-heralded

Sky Gondola, causing several of its vulnerable cars to come crashing to the ground. As the police statement noted dryly, "innocent people could have died."

The gondola venture was — and still is — a key part of Homage's drive to attract tourists by whisking them up to the top of one of the world's largest granite monoliths and showing them stunning views of the coastal mountains all around … and, of course, the ethereal Pacific Ocean below.

But the chairlift had drawn the ire of eco-activists, weekend warriors, and others who still seemed to believe in the concept of a pristine wilderness, untouched by human hands. They ignored the fact that people, especially American Indians, had been interacting with nature for thousands of years. Managed wilderness, according to the so-called experts, was the more sensible and realistic norm now.

Cabbie Dale, meanwhile, told me he sided with animal-rights groups who had recently disrupted an SPCA fundraising event while protesting against "widespread cruelty" in current farming practices. I knew this because one day when Chelsea had borrowed my truck, I spent a half-hour discussing it with Dale in his electric-powered taxi on my way to see friends of mine on the other side of Homage.

Dale confirmed to me what I'd already heard from others, namely that he was originally from New York, had a PhD in engineering, and had once worked at a Boston-based aerospace firm that designed and manufactured missile systems. But he had become fed up with the dismissive way in which he was treated if he questioned anything … and was regularly blamed for any and every ensuing mishap.

Oh, and he had been forced to rethink his views about marriage, which he didn't feel was serving humanity well and had stripped him of most of his savings.

"Yes, divorce is hell. I know that only too well from my experience," I said. "But what caused you to change your mind about all the other stuff, including your strong views on animal liberation and eco-extremism?"

"Well, a combination of things, including my realization that the way the world is going, it could all end soon," he said. "And I didn't want to think I'd done nothing about it. Also, I have gotten to know some of the activists here. And they seem fine, committed people. I drive them around all the time."

"You mean they have enough money to ferry themselves around in taxis," I asked, a little incredulous.

"Yes, they are normal people, like you and me. They just think it's better to have fewer cars and trucks on the road … and fewer giant, energy-sucking gondolas."

"I guess normality is in the eye of the beholder," I said. "But I don't see how causing millions of dollars of damage by sabotaging other people's property — and potentially endangering their lives — is normal. I mean, I've had to spend thousands of dollars on a new security system at the lodge, money I can ill afford, just because some excited urbanites seem to think it's wrong for me to keep farm animals."

And there the conversation slowed to a halt. Charming as Dale appeared behind the wheel, I understood then and there that we probably would never see eye to eye — even though I respected him as someone who was his own person and didn't simply follow the tribe in lemming-like fashion.

More recently, I had cause to observe Dale at work off the road … at Sandy's place. He perhaps didn't see me, but I spotted him out-front, unloading a trunk-full of trash bags and hauling them into the barn, where they were mysteriously swallowed.

Sandy was out there to watch over Dale. I was sure of that. But my supposed boyfriend refused to answer when I later questioned him about what exactly was in those bags. All he would say is, "Dale and I, we're in business together. I do business with lots of people in the valley, just like you do. I don't have good wheels at the moment, so I rely on Dale for my transportation, just like everyone else in the valley does."

The bottom line, though, was that Sandy and I had run into a roadblock, at least as far as our romantic relationship was concerned. From all I'd heard and seen with my own eyes, he was mixed up with drugs or other doubtful stuff. And I certainly didn't want Jess to become involved in that in any way. For my daughter and only child, I now wanted only blue skies and plain sailing.

Also, I didn't like what I'd heard about his son Joel. However well the youth interacted with my lodge guests out on the mountain bike trails, he clearly had a nasty streak. And I feared Jess might be persuaded to make the same mistake as I had … by succumbing to a pushy, persistent man's amorous advances and winding up pregnant, bullied, and otherwise abused.

My own marriage to Rory had started out well, with a series of challenging pack trips, hard partying, and spine-tingling sex. And we seemed to have a love of horses in common. But it disintegrated into prolonged name-calling any time I challenged his views, say, on the right schooling for Jess … or the supposed fact that socialists are ugly-looking.

When I pointed out to Rory that some of the most handsome Hollywood actors were, in fact, card-carrying lefties, he would explode with anger — and either punch a hole in the wall or hit me. I soon learned to keep my mouth shut.

Rory was a charismatic man. And everybody figured he'd be a big success. He had the looks, the drive … and the schooling. And he seemed fearless. He had a good university degree, and was planning to follow in his father's footsteps in the gilded offices of the oil industry. But he also loved the outdoors and wanted to be a rancher and hunting guide. That, in fact, is what drew us together.

Above all, Rory was determined to be his own man. Which is what he was, until it all became too much for him.

The winters with him were especially bad. He started to drink more and rile people up more with his bluntness and belligerence. He became the bully he always accused his father of being. And I became his punching bag … and the victim of his verbal lash.

The final straw for me was when he started to turn on Jess, whom he insisted he really loved, by criticizing and chastising her for absolutely everything. I knew then we had to get out of there at once while Jess and I were still in one piece. And that's what we did. Believe me, it wasn't easy, though my parents did what they could to help.

Some years after I left him, I heard he was depressed and lonely, and his drinking and womanizing had gotten worse. One especially cold winter evening, he apparently went to town and got into a bar fight that spilled out onto the street. I still don't know the full details. But he was glassed in the face, knocked unconscious, and lay on the ground …until he literally froze to death.

One of the hardest things I ever had to do was tell Jess that her seemingly indestructible father had died, and that I had stayed with him for far too long. He needed serious help, I said, which I was unable to give him.

Bullying, I have since learned, is often passed down through the generations. And there is little you can do about it — except put as much daylight as you can between yourself and it. At least that's what I did. Eventually.

CHAPTER 9

CHANGE

Newsman Nick Tomalin famously said that the only qualities essential for success in journalism are "rat-like cunning, a plausible manner, and a little literary ability."

Blacksmith Sandy may not have been a wordsmith or overly interested in literature, but he more than made up for this with his other two qualities. He cunningly and plausibly skated through life by charming everyone he met. Or almost everyone.

As far as I knew, Sandy never wanted to be involved in any way with the news business. He was someone who shunned the limelight. He was downright secretive, in fact, refusing to talk about his checkered past or hoped-for future, except in the most general of terms.

The last absolutely honest thing he said to me, I suspect, was that I asked too many questions, and took too many photographs. I couldn't disagree with him. I have always been a bit of a busybody. I even took a course in investigative journalism in the hope that one day I could be a real writer, not simply a passive reader and note-taker.

Instead, I wound up as a freelance shutterbug, shooting everything from intimate portraits and headshots to weddings and corporate annual meetings. I kept on looking at life through some kind of prying lens. And I have never stopped being grateful to my parents for giving me a rudimentary camera on my fourteenth birthday. They told me to "go outside, look around, and snap the best pictures you can find."

In other words, they were telling me to be creative. As black-and-white eco-photographer Ansel Adams said, "you don't take a photograph, you make it." And you make it by treating your potential subjects with singular respect, not simply intrusive curiosity.

The picture I'm still most proud of is of my mother looking out the kitchen window … in the most inquisitive manner. After I took the shot, I asked her why she looked so incredulous. "I just saw a cougar out there by the aspens," she said. Later, I entered the picture in a local library competition and won a ribbon "for capturing a moment of wonderment."

One thing I did respect about Sandy was his ease with horses — a quality he'd obviously inherited from his Irish farrier father and one which I wish he'd been able to pass onto his son Joel. I realize now it was not so much the physical attraction between us that brought us together, but our ability to talk to each other about horses, my enduring passion.

After a while, though, Sandy seemed to tire of that, telling me that horses were difficult and expensive to keep and moody as mountains, as if both traits held the key to his prolonged distress.

We agreed, though, to remain friends. And the break-up didn't surprise my best friend Carrie, who worked as an assistant manager in a Homage bank. She said she didn't know what had attracted me to Sandy in the first place, "except his lean bod and country drawl."

She suggested that, if I wanted a new man, I should sign up to a dating site, and meet men in a more practical, methodical way. "Everyone's doing it," she said.

I told Carrie I thought everyone was nuts, though I'd heard of one website that let women do background checks on men and anonymously share "red flag" behavior.

"That sounds very sensible," she said. "So why don't you give it a try? I can always help you check a prospect out and at least see if he has two cents to his name."

I said I wasn't wanting or hoping to land a millionaire, just someone who was employed, dependable and able to help shoulder the load at the lodge.

"Forget the lodge for the moment," Carrie advised. "What you need to do is to enjoy yourself. You deserve it. You've been through hell with all you've had to deal with."

I told her I was far too busy to start dating right away, to which she replied, "You're never too busy to be kind … and never too busy to fall in love."

Joel, meanwhile, continued to work at the lodge, despite my misgivings about his rough approach to horses and what I felt might possibly be his creeping obsession with Jess. Was I again being too selectively indifferent?

The lodge visitors, though, clearly loved Joel's full-day and half-day bike rides on the "gnarly" mountains trails. Also, the revenue from this was very welcome. And the guests seemed to suffer fewer injuries from biking with him than riding the rented horses just down the road.

One day at the barn, I congratulated Joel about this, saying I was pleased he seemed to be working well with Jess. But I reminded him as delicately as I could that she already had a boyfriend, namely Matt. Also, Matt would soon be returning for some rest and recuperation after an intense stint on the major North American mountain-biking circuit.

"I've talked to Matt about him helping us out at the lodge for a while," I said, leaning casually on the barn door. "And he says he is interested in joining you in leading the rides from the lodge. They've become quite popular. So, I hope you two will get along."

"That will be more up to him than me," Joel said, scowling. "Matt's a good bike rider, and he could be a good friend. The trouble is his ego often gets in the way. Just ask anybody who's been to school with him. Besides, I don't like the way he treats Jess."

"What exactly do you mean by that?" I asked, my hackles rising.

"Matt has a reputation as a womanizer," he replied, not beating around the bush. "And whenever he's in this part of the world, which is rare these days, he parades around as if he owns the place. I can see how it hurts Jess. She doesn't like to see pictures of him with, well, groupies."

"Well, I'm sorry to hear that. But let's make sure there's no conflict between you and Matt, especially when the guests are around."

Given the beauty of the valley, though, I expected the guests would always be around … like the river. At least if I could help it. They'd return every spring and fall, like migrating birds.

It was the valley residents, especially the long-term ones, I was more worried about. They had come to Maverick Valley because of the fun, freedom, and inspiration it offered. But change had now come calling for them in the form of the mega-resort that was about to slap them in the face. And just like a once-in-a-generation flood triggered by a surging Homage River, they wouldn't know what had hit them … until they were well and truly swamped.

CHAPTER 10

JESS

Of all the people I've had serious concerns about in my checkered life, the one who has worried me the most is Jess, my lovely daughter, now nineteen, the special one with the sad green eyes and free-flowing, dark-brown hair.

Well, you'll say, that's what all mothers do. They obsess over their kids, especially those who are lonely only children. But ever since she was born two months premature, wild Jess had always lived on the edge or pushed toward some kind of extreme.

Whether climbing a tree, hanging upside down from a chair, or sliding down steep, slippery gravel slopes, she had been testing boundaries, especially those involving her looks and fashion. And she could be overly moody and pouty … and all wrapped up in herself.

It wasn't her fault. Her father was often overbearing and frighteningly explosive, and Jess was determined to stand up to him … or out from him. The result was she sometimes drew the wrong kind of attention from the wrong type of people. My job was to steer her on the right course so she would stop becoming a hellion and avoid getting into serious, long-term trouble.

I also knew that Jess could be sweet and loving. One day when she was eleven and we had gone for a hike, we came across a fawn that was either orphaned or had temporarily lost its mother. We waited around to see if the mother would return. Then, we moved in. And I was so proud of the way Jess went into rescue mode and slowly, quietly, and instinctively knew how to approach this delicate, lost creature.

"Mum, we need to take it to the animal shelter," she said. Which is just what we did. And Jess later checked in at the shelter to see how the fawn was progressing. It survived, and was later released to the wild with other orphaned deer.

So, I was overjoyed Jess was getting on well with the bubbly, down-to-earth Chelsea, who also loved animals and was using the summer at the lodge to further her vet studies in the best possible way … by gaining day-to-day experience with all the creatures we had to care for there.

Jess also helped Chelsea with a project I had nothing to do with, namely the creation of a children's sanctuary in the woods bordering the pasture. It was a magical, hobbit-like hideaway, featuring fairy rock puzzles, moss-leaf-and-pinecone circles, and painted tree houses. It even had a little theater, complete with miniature log benches.

Unlike the equable Chelsea, though, Jess was undoubtedly an up-and-down person. Even before she was in her teens, she either excelled at a school subject or she flunked it. She either wore body-hugging jeans or balloon-like dresses. She put on too much makeup or none at all.

Moderation wasn't in her vocabulary. And I wasn't too surprised when one day she came back with a tattoo on her right lower ankle — a little deer — and announced she wanted to add to that tat soon.

Though rarely boring herself, Jess was easily bored, especially by most of the local lads who had little or nothing to say for themselves, but somehow relished being, well, sex pests.

I was even beginning to think she might be gay … at least until she had suddenly opened up to me about how Matt was now her boyfriend. She confirmed he was a twenty-year-old champion mountain-biker who was bold, brash, and super-confident. Like father, like daughter — that was my initial reaction.

I did worry, though, when she came back late from a trail ride one afternoon with Matt, looking as if she'd spent the afternoon in a wind tunnel.

I was disappointed, too, when my friend Carrie reiterated what Joel had said, namely that Matt was reported to be a player and a babe magnet, like Jess's dad used to be. Oh no, I thought.

I tried not to be too judgmental, and to remind myself of the saying that "rumors are passed by haters, spread by fools, and believed by idiots." I also knew that Jess was nothing if not determined … and had already beaten the odds by securing a place at university.

Jess now insisted that, like Chelsea, who was three years older than her and a kind of mentor, she wanted to become a vet. And armed with a clear direction, it was her life to lead as the enterprising, elbows-out young woman I always hoped she would be.

That night, though, Jess returned in tears, saying she'd had a row with Matt. She explained that, after an afternoon on the trails and an evening at the lodge, the two of them went to the Roadhouse Club in Homage for a night cap when they ran into Joel and a group of his pals.

Unpleasantries were exchanged between the two young men and a fight broke out, which the bouncers were quick to break up. But some physical damage was done, some blood spilled, and sheriff's deputies were called.

I tried not to be too judgmental, but just to listen to what Jess had to say. She was obviously in a mood to talk … and to unload some of the heavy baggage she had been carrying.

"I like Joel, and I'm flattered that he really likes me and listens to what I say," she said. "But I don't trust him and his moods, especially around horses. He seems so negative a lot of the time, and has a chip on his shoulder."

Jess paused, sighed, and continued: "As for Matt, he's super cocky and that's appealing, given all the geeks and nerds around here these days. But I don't really think he's the one for me, as he still has a lot of competing to do — and a great deal of growing up. But he's fun to be with, at least when Joel isn't around."

"I know you'll sort it all out," I replied. "Just trust your instincts and listen to your inner voice."

"How come you didn't always trust yours?"

"Yes, you're right," I said. "I put up with too much from too many people for too long. I was a people-pleaser. And I learned the hard way that is not the way to live. I should have trusted my gut back then. And it would have spared me — and you — a ton of grief. I'm really sorry for that."

"Yes, I wish we hadn't taken so long to get our act together as a family," Jess said.

"You're right. It's good to keep life simple and uncomplicated. But that's not always achievable. In any case, I hope you can learn from my mistakes … and do things better."

"I hope so, too. But I have to say I'm still having a hard time dealing with men."

"You remind me a lot of what I was like when I first met your father, and was conflicted over the attention from two handsome, eager young men. One was volatile, with all the charisma in the world. The other was a steady Eddie, who was shy and penniless, but had a heart of gold. Now, I'd just like to have someone who can help me fix the lodge!"

"You'll find someone, mother. I know you will. You always do," Jess said. "And thanks for listening to me tonight. I really needed your support."

CHAPTER 11

UP AND DOWN

Watched over by sky-scraping mountains and sheer granite cliffs, Maverick Valley is widely known for its varied alpine climbing and close-knit, rock-climbing community.

While dedicated mountain-bikers huck and hurl themselves down its impossibly steep slopes and tortuous routes, committed mountaineers clamber and claw their way up them.

Matt was addicted to both high-adrenalin sports. And that day, he was obviously determined to show off his extraordinary extreme skills to Jess, his so-called steady girlfriend … and, if possible, to school her in them.

What Matt had told me earlier he really liked about my daughter was that she was outdoor-minded and always seemed up for adventure. What he didn't like, he said, was her sudden, unexpected outbursts of temper.

One of those eruptions was clearly what provoked a nasty but apparently not unusual argument between them as he tried to guide her up a cliff on the lower reaches of Shadow Mountain.

"Don't treat me like I'm one of your little groupies," was the gist of what Jess was later overheard screaming. "I can figure things out on my own. I'm a big girl now."

"Jess, I'm just trying to help," Matt was heard replying. "Why do you take everything the wrong way?"

The ensuing yelling echoed loudly around the forested trails. It even stopped four local mountain-bikers in their tracks. Days later, when questioned about it by police, the bikers recalled the brouhaha in vivid detail, and even admitted they had a good laugh about it. "Those who climb together, fall together … or fall out together," quipped one of them.

From what I pieced together later, a period of relative calm ensued as Jess harrumphed her way down the mountain.

Matt, on the other hand, made his way to the nearest large, relatively flat rock ledge to cool down and maybe engage in some marijuana-enhanced meditation.

He must have sensed there was no point waiting around for his moody girlfriend to calm herself and come around to his way of thinking. Better to let her know he was not impressed … and not prepared to be pushed around.

Matt clearly felt he didn't need any more stress and aggravation from what was supposed to be a relaxing, reinvigorating vacation. And I think he must either have fallen into some kind of trance as he stared out at the bank of fluffy clouds and sun-kissed mountains across the valley … or had just gone to sleep.

One of the passing bikers later told police he thought he saw a "climber type" hunched over on a cliff near the single-track trail they themselves were taking … and the person looked "either exhausted or stoned."

Personally, I don't know how you can tell at a distance if someone is stoned, but it is a safe assumption in these parts that they might well be. At least if they're stationary.

Joel, meanwhile, was stewing as per usual. He'd taken out a group of mountain-bikers in the morning and had since busied himself at the lodge, catching up on his billings and answering a million questions from demanding visitors.

He certainly didn't like the thought that Jess and Matt were out together renewing their relationship and otherwise having fun, while he was having to work like a galley slave for a pittance.

Finally, Joel's inquisitiveness got the better of him and he decided it was time to get a little exercise … and to get rid of his hangover. He headed out on his bike to the cliff face where Jess had told him she would be climbing with Matt.

Joel told me he planned to apologize to Matt for his behavior the previous night at the club. But he also insisted he didn't, in fact, see either Matt or Jess on the mountain. So, he returned to the barn to attend to Chester, the steady horse I had hoped he would learn to treat well, and then tidy up for the day.

I met Joel as he was leaving for his father's place, and asked him whether he had seen Jess. "No, I haven't," he said. "I guess she's still on her climbing date with Matt. Or maybe she's off in a funk. In any case, she's not in the habit of informing me of her whereabouts these days."

I sympathized with him. But I told him in no uncertain terms that he and Jess must try harder to get along and not let their little spats affect the way they did their work or treated the guests. I stressed they were not in competition with each other to see who could be the most mean and miserable.

"People from the city pay good money to come here because they want to avoid ugly confrontations and commotions," I explained. "They want to think of us country people as happy people who have smiles on our faces and are willing to please … not as irate rednecks and grumpy sourpusses."

"I suppose they can always dream," replied Joel, "or go to some fancy resort in Florida where they pay the staff three times as much … as well as tipping them like kings."

I let that zinger go. But I was starting to think I had to stop treating Joel with kid gloves. I was his boss, responsible for all the lodge operations. And what he needed right now from his employer in the worst way were some boundaries. So did his father, for that matter.

Jess showed up at the lodge soon after, in no apparent physical or mental discomfort. But she went straight to her cabin for the evening. And, when I called her on her cellphone, all she could say was that she'd had an argument with Matt — and didn't want to discuss it further.

"But where's Matt?" I asked. "Nobody seems to have seen him."

"Who knows," she replied. "He's a big boy now and can take care of himself."

Given the circumstances, I had to agree with her. Matt was nothing if not a tough, competitive, self-reliant young man in the prime of his life. He could well look after himself.

CHAPTER 12

LONG TIME NO SEE!

Shopping on main street in downtown Homage is a little like preparing for your wedding. You can always find something old, something new, something borrowed, and something blue.

Jane's Interiors is a perfect example of this. There were invariably items that made you look twice, whether a vintage desk, modern couch, much-owned painting, blue table lamp … or just some dried flowers and a walking stick. You never knew what you were going to get. All second hand.

I had dropped into the store for no particular reason, except that it was close to where I could find free parking, which was in short supply now that condo buildings were going up everywhere. And I was fidgeting aimlessly with a couple of decorative pillows when I ran into someone I hadn't seen for nearly twenty years.

Clad in a two-tone sheriff's uniform, he strode up to the counter as purposefully as if he were about to play the final hole of a major golf tournament.

He shook hands with the storeowner, saying: "Hi, Jane. I was passing by and heard about the robbery. Tell me all about it, and we'll see what we can do."

Jane, who looked as if she had recently been involved in hand-to-hand combat with a berserk burglar, unloaded on him.

"You know what bothers me," she said. "It's that the crime in this county is getting worse … far worse, what with the drugs, the street fights, the broken windows and all the break-ins. And I want to know what you police are doing about it."

"Well, let's just say we're trying hard," Luke said, smiling now. "And if you vote for me in the fall, I can assure you that we will try even harder."

Just then, we all heard a loud bang outside on the street, as if the crime wave had resumed. And while it turned out to be construction noise up the street, the sheriff turned around so he faced me directly.

In an instant, I confirmed that he was, indeed, Luke, the hunky ranch hand who'd had a crush on me when I was twenty and working as a starry-eyed kid wrangler.

"Wow, I don't believe it. How time flies, Sheriff Luke," I said, staring into his deep blues.

"But you still look as beautiful as ever, Kyra," he replied smoothly, confidently.

"You look well yourself, though I imagine you're no longer mending ranch fences and racing horses across irrigation ditches."

"No, I don't have the time or energy to race horses, but I'm still mending fences, so to speak," Luke laughed, leaning in a little.

"I've got to go now," I lied, handing him my business card. "But we should have a coffee some time and catch up. Give me a shout at the lodge."

"Yes, I heard that you'd taken that over. Good for you … but I'm sorry to hear about your dad."

"Thank you. It's been a difficult time for my daughter Jess and me. But we're getting back on our feet again. I hope things are good for you."

"I'm doing okay, thanks. But I have my hands full with all that's going on in the area … as Jane here will tell you."

"Yes, I'd better leave you now with Jane. She has more pressing issues. But let's not forget to have that catch-up coffee some time soon."

I walked out the door, turned and called out: "Bye, Jane I'll be in again soon. You have lovely things."

Returning to my truck, I blushed and shuddered a little, realizing that seeing Luke again had filled me with bubbly anticipation — about a surge of possibilities to come.

By the time I returned to the lodge, I had gone over some reunion-with-Luke questions a hundred times in my head. Was it fate or blind luck? I mean, what were the chances of meeting him like that, and after all this time?

Why was I so flustered, standing there lamely with a fluffy red pillow in my hand? And why did I break off our chat so quickly? Why was I more worried about Jane than myself?

Someday, I have to figure out why it is that, despite being an incurable romantic, I'm always so eager to avoid intense feelings and emotions … and prolong loneliness? I mean it's not as if have a ton of male friends in Maverick Valley.

Luke did call, a few days later, and suggested we meet at the Sundance Café, which would work better for him than the lodge as it was closer to his office. He feared he might be called away in the event of an emergency.

I was quick to agree to this neutral venue, as I didn't think I knew him well enough to host him at the lodge. That kind of potentially awkward visit, with all the preparation required, was just too early in this slow dance.

Besides, the Sundance really was the best place to meet … on the edge of the valley but reasonably close to town. It had great coffee and had avoided the modern trend toward scowling, robotic servers who expect you to spell out your order in some overly programmed way. It also offered physical room to breathe.

Luke arrived on time and looked cool and fresh in smart jeans and a white dress shirt. I wore a turquoise top, navy-blue pants and handmade, silver-hoop earrings. My hair was up and a little tousled. And I added a touch of blush and lip tint for a casual chic look. Inside, I was bubbling with excitement.

What surprised me, though, was that Luke didn't seem keen to rehash old times or dwell on the way I once dumped him for an older, richer, angrier man. He wanted instead to warn me about Sandy, something he said he should have done months ago when he heard that "I had been shacked up with him."

I corrected him at once, saying I had never moved in with Sandy, and that the relationship, puzzling and troubled as it was, was now over.

"Good, because I want you to know in the strictest confidence that we have had him and his son Joel under surveillance. That too is now over, but I felt I should tell you on the down-low I don't think he is a good person or someone you or your daughter should associate with."

"What do you mean 'not a good person'?"

"Well, all indications are that he is involved in criminal activity involving drugs … and possibly underage girls. And again, I must stress that you didn't hear this from me."

"Oh, for heaven's sake, Luke, come down from your high horse. Tell me the score."

"Well, we have footage of you on camera at his place. We also have footage of Jess and Joel at the Roadhouse Club where Sandy is a silent partner. I'm warning you to be careful, and I think you should also warn Jess about both him and Joel."

"I wish you had told me this earlier, Luke. But thanks for doing so now. I hope the video won't hurt my business in any way."

"No, it won't. And I just hope you'll inform me if, moving forward, you see or hear something untoward. Joel works part-time at the lodge, doesn't he?"

"Yes, he does," I said. "And he's a good worker, though his personality could use some improvement."

As for the fence-mending sheriff, I had to admit he did a terrific job playing the role of concerned cop. But I would have liked to have seen more of his human side, which would now have to wait for yet another day.

With Luke it was becoming clear that you never quite knew what you were going to get. Our get-together was far different from the coffee catch-up I had envisaged. It was more a "heads-up, watch-your-back" session. But let's just say my interest was still perked.

CHAPTER 13

VANISHING ACT

Sheriff Luke came round to the lodge sooner than I thought he would … to interview Jess about Matt going missing.

Apparently, no one had seen Matt for days. And his agent in Seattle was "very concerned," because he had a bunch of media interviews lined up for him … ones he was loathe to turn down, at least if his client "really wanted to make it to the big time."

Jess confirmed to Luke that she and Matt, who was supposed to be having some down time for the week, had gotten into a row while out rock climbing above the lodge.

"It was stupid really," she said. "Matt was being insufferably chauvinistic, as per usual, and for once I wasn't prepared to sit there and take it. I'd had enough of his arrogance."

"So, what did you and he do then?" Luke said.

"I just made my way slowly back down to the lodge … and laid down in my cabin to clear my head and put my nose in my books. Then, I went to help Chelsea feed the animals, again as per usual. Just ask Mom or Joel."

"And what did Matt do?" the sheriff continued.

"I don't know. I really don't know. I was hoping to see him later so we could have a long hard talk about our relationship and whether he thought, as I do, that it was heading over a cliff, if you can excuse the pun."

"Well, Jess, as you may already know, a group of bikers on the mountain told deputies they'd heard you and him carrying on and generally having a nasty argument," Luke said. "They stressed it was very loud and sounded as if it might have turned physical. According to the written notes I have of our interviews with them, you allegedly said, 'Don't touch me, and do that again and I'll kill you.'"

"So, Sheriff, you are treating me as some kind of suspect," Jess said, as if shocked by the notion, "even though he was the one who touched me."

"At least until Matt shows up and checks in and tells us his version of what went on and where he went," Luke replied in an official, monotone way.

"From what I know, that'll be sooner rather than later," Jess suggested. "Whenever Matt's in a sulk, he has a habit of taking off. And when the time's right for him, he reappears out of the blue as right as rain."

"Well, the list of people who haven't heard from him is growing," Luke said. "Let me know the moment you hear something. In the meantime, don't go anywhere where we can't contact you. And stay safe. Send my regards to your mother."

In the meantime, neither Sandy or Joel said they had heard or seen anything of Matt. "He likes to do a vanishing act from time to time to make himself feel important," was all the surly Joel would say.

Later that day, I was giving a speech on behalf of the Save Maverick Valley Coalition to the local Community Services Society. Nobody I ran into had seen him. They all said he was a free spirit who did just what he liked. They didn't really know what Jess saw in him … except, of course, for his fame, great looks, and obvious personal magnetism.

As for my crusading speech, it seemed to be well-received, though it was hard to tell whether we in the Coalition really were winning our fight to save the community from the proposed new mega-resort.

I reminded the packed village hall that the massive development, when fully built out, would include three eight-storey hotels with hundreds of condos, at least 40 villas and 50 single-family homes, a restaurant, a pier-cum-marina on the river, a spa … and so on and so on.

Besides, the construction of the futuristic project, which looked completely out of character for Maverick Valley, was to be centered around an old, empty, government-run sanitorium that was said to be riddled with asbestos. Cleaning all that up could disrupt the community for years.

"This will totally transform the valley and threaten everything we love about living here," I concluded. "It's time for us all to stand up and be counted."

Locals I knew told me afterwards that I had given a rousing, inspirational speech that was long overdue. They said they were concerned about everything from gridlock on the narrow, winding road through the valley to increased boat traffic on the river.

But, if I'm honest, the cheers weren't as loud as I had expected. And I have learned the hard way that, in the battle between development and environment, money often talks the loudest.

One middle-aged audience member called John, whom I strongly suspected of being a corporate plant, suggested our community desperately needed the services the project would provide. He described it as "smart growth," using the current jargon to describe high-density development designed to reduce environmental impacts.

"We can't be a backwater for ever. We have to move with the times," John noted.

"By all means, move with the times, but let's not allow Peregrine Holdings to constrict and crush us," I replied.

"This is hardly a case of being crushed by anyone. We live in a vast, remote area," he said. "This will affect only one small part of it."

"It's one key part of the whole," I replied. "It's at the very entrance to the valley."

"Yes, it's at the edge of it … where it can be easily controlled and managed. Besides, Kyra, don't you have a serious conflict-of-interest here? I mean, aren't you opposed to it simply because you fear it'll compete with your own lodge for tourist dollars?"

"I welcome competition, provided it's on a level playing field," I said. "But I don't think we need more 'services' like the 'ethical escort service' that opened up the other day calling itself Eden Escorts. I mean, what kind of Eden is that … and on what scale?"

I continued. "I think most of us in this village hall would agree that the 'ethical' thing to do would be to scale down this scary development, which is way over the top. We're here to escape the noise, bustle, and crime of big-city life, not invite big-city congestion to come and camp right here on our doorstep."

"You talk of crime," John repeated in his condescending way. "But you already have all the drugs and the crime you'll ever need right here. And if you don't believe me, ask the sheriff. He'll tell you it's never been as bad as it is right now."

John added, "The scourge of fentanyl is at your door, plus all the weed, heroin, and cocaine that people can stuff into their backpacks. Just look around you."

The image of Sandy moving trash bags into his barn suddenly popped back into my head. And from all I'd been hearing and seeing of late, I'd grudgingly had to agree with John that the current state of community safety in Maverick Valley was hardly reassuring.

Indeed, statistics showed the incidence of violent crime was generally even higher than in nearby urban areas.

But that was a conversation for another day … hopefully with Luke involved.

CHAPTER 14

LIFE AND DEATH

When a group of river rafters spotted a body in Homage River in Maverick Valley, media reports didn't immediately convey a sense of great surprise. The powerful river and its torrential tributaries had claimed many lives over the years in a mercurial, mountainous land accustomed to fires, floods, and other extremes of nature's wrath.

Humans in the area, too, seemed larger than life. They were loud talkers, big dreamers, and huge risk-takers ... not simply safety-obsessed, second-home owners.

People died when they fell into the river, went swimming or boating in it ... or drove into it stoned or drunk. Sometimes they were never found, especially when search-and-rescue efforts were hampered by what were politely called "hazardous" or "treacherous" conditions.

The battered body found wedged between two large rocks on a bend in the river near Hangman Falls was clearly that of a young man who had recently suffered several broken bones and other severe trauma.

The only real issue was whether these disfiguring injuries were caused by falling from a great height or out of a car or a boat. Or not from a fall at all. It could be he was the victim of a serious crime.

That determination would ultimately be made by a coroner or medical examiner trained in forensic pathology. There were no obvious signs of decomposition. Indeed, initial reports suggested to the sheriff's office that the body was indeed that of Matt, the missing mountain-bike star recently seen arguing loudly with his girlfriend Jess on the lower reaches of Shadow Mountain.

Follow-up media reports then began to focus on how unusual — and especially tragic — it was for a top young athlete and experienced outdoorsman in the prime of his life to meet his maker in this way. Was he really as cool and self-confident as he was always cracked up to be?

"Do they think it was suicide," was the first question I asked Luke, when he phoned to say he was planning to stop by at the lodge in an hour or so.

"No, but they haven't ruled it out. And it's one of the things I'd like to talk to Jess and you about," Luke said. "I know he took drugs. Many young people seem to do that these days. But did he ever appear depressed or have a history of depression in his family? In any case, please think about it and let me know when I'm there."

Jess, as you can imagine, was now a complete mess and reluctant to be reinterviewed by Luke. But I told her that, given all the rumors going around about her involvement, it would be better if she let the sheriff know as many of the facts as possible … and also learn from him what the cops think might have happened.

Luke was respectful, but firm with Jess. He wanted to know exactly what was said and who said it on her climb with Matt, and whether he had ever talked to her about possibly wanting to kill himself.

"He never said anything like that," Jess replied. "But he did say one time he was tired of me always accusing him of being brash, overconfident, and a bit of a bully. He said that wasn't him at all, but professional mountain-bike racing demanded you have total belief in yourself. Uncertainty and indecision were for losers."

"You mean, he had to put on some kind of an act in other words?"

"Yes, I guess. But it was an act I was getting tired of. And I told him so. And now I wish I hadn't. It all seems so terribly silly — and sad. Terribly sad. I can't believe I won't see him again. Ever."

Luke moved in to comfort her. But she wasn't finished.

"And I won't be able to hold him in my arms," Jess said. "What a stupid way to die, especially at his age and time of life, with everything to live for. I really loved that guy. He was a one-of-a-kind man in every sense of the word. And I didn't even have time to tell him that … or even wish him goodbye."

With that, Jess teared up, sobbed, and returned to her cabin to continue to cope further with her loss. And I had a one-on-one with Luke that went on for over an hour ... one in which he opened up to me about a lot of things, including the time we were together years ago when "that young dude" had died on one of my kiddie rides.

"I should have been there for you more then," he confessed. "I was self-centered then and I know it. But you also seemed a bit standoffish. And I thought you just wanted to be alone … or with Rory."

"No worries," I said. "I totally understand. We all had a lot of growing up to do. And it seems like it was such a different era, more carefree in a way, but maybe crueler."

"It's a funny thing," Luke continued, "but when I was at the hospital in Homage the other day, I ran into the father of the boy who died on that ride. He's some kind of senior doctor there. He seemed like a real nice guy."

"How amazing," I replied, dumbstruck that this should now come back to haunt me, just as I was becoming my own person again.

"And, no, the doctor doesn't hold you or anyone else responsible," Luke replied. "He described it to me as 'just one of those tragic accidents.'"

"Wow," I said. "He's a decent, mature-thinking kind of guy. But I guess he has seen quite a bit of life and death and other turmoil in his medical life."

"He did say, though, that the boy's older brother, Simon, had been fooling around with a handheld noisemaker at the time, and that may have spooked the horse."

"A noisemaker?"

"One of those spinning ratchets kids love. I think you can even get ones that mimic the nickering and neighing of horses."

"Yes, come to think of it, I've heard of them."

"In any case, you can ask him about it," Luke said. "He gave me his card and said he and his wife—she's a nurse at the hospital—would be happy to talk to you about it. Give them a call or, better still, go see them. I'm sure they'd appreciate it, with all they've been through."

I didn't know whether to laugh or cry. First, Matt's horrible death and now this, a bolt from the blue. When would the drama ever end? Was this the curse of living in this valley, that you could never go there to escape your past, as so many of us hoped?

Despite reassurances to the contrary, I had felt guilty about that young horse rider's death for years, not least because I had failed to have a good long talk to his parents at the time of the tragedy.

I also hadn't followed up to see how their family was doing. I had been selfish, thinking only of my own predicament.

But life was full of second chances. And it was time I took them. I hoped Jess would do so, too, in her own search for meaning and purpose in life — and love.

CHAPTER 15

AGING WELL

I called the number on the card Luke had given me, and asked for Dr. Peter Handsworth, an orthopedic surgeon at Homage Hospital. He didn't pick up right away, but phoned back much sooner than I'd expected.

"Thank you for calling, Kyra. Kind of you. Do you have a moment to talk?"

"Yes, of course. I'm so sorry I haven't phoned before, but I wasn't aware you were in town."

"No need to apologize. Alice and I have been meaning to get in touch, ever since we arrived here last year. So has our son, Simon. You may remember him. He's interning at the hospital."

"That's amazing … I mean him being a doctor now. You must be proud. He must be nearly 30."

"Actually he's 28, going on 29. But he's all grown up, I can assure you. And I couldn't have wished for a better son."

"Wow, how time flies. I'm not going to reveal my age. But my daughter, Jess, is now 20."

"Yes, the sheriff told me she was about to go university after taking a year out to help you set up operations at your Maverick Valley lodge."

"Luke is right, as usual. Jess wants to be a vet, and is learning animal care from the ground up here. But you and Alice — and Simon, of course — must come and visit us. The lodge could still use some work, but it's a lovely setting, one I never tire of. And the food is aways fresh."

"Well, that's a tempting offer. But, if it's okay with you, why don't we meet first somewhere in town? I'm often on call, so it's easier for us to stay close to the hospital. Alice is a nurse here, too, as you may already know."

"Do you have a particular place in mind?"

"How about seven o'clock on Friday at the Waterview Grill? I'll book now, as it often gets very busy."

"I much look forward to seeing you then," I replied, glad at the newfound urgency with which Dr. Peter seemed to want a sit-down meeting. The need for one had been hanging over me for years. I just hoped it wouldn't come with any unwelcome surprises: legal, medical, or otherwise.

But there didn't appear to be any nasty hiccups as we settled into wild salmon and other seafood.

The restaurant overlooked one of the most photographed bends in the Homage River, directly opposite to where scores of bald eagles congregate each winter to nest and breed.

Dr. Peter wore an open-neck, light-blue shirt and navy-blue pants. Alice, looking elegantly casual in a pale pink blouse, black pencil skirt with sensible low heels. She had a grey cashmere scarf loosely draped around her neck and shoulders.

Both had clearly aged somewhat. Yet, they were just as polite and understanding — and non-accusatory — as they were 18 years ago when their younger son, seven-year-old Alex, died on one of my trail rides. And they graciously avoided any discussion of that distressing event until I myself brought it up during dessert.

In the meantime, they picked my brains on everything from the annual arrival of the eagles to the pervasiveness of illegal drug use in Homage and the controversial new real-estate project planned for Maverick Valley.

I told them that I might be biased, but I thought the development, as currently proposed, would be a disaster, disrupting the quaint, quirky, homey feel of the valley that residents and visitors alike loved so much. And it would encourage sport tourism to expand to mass tourism, ruining the whole character of this special place with its soaring mountains, scenic canyons, and magical wilderness.

"Change comes to everything," I said. "I understand that. But I for one prefer evolution to revolution. It's so much less disruptive."

Alice agreed. "One of the reasons we came to this part of the world," she said, "was to give Simon and ourselves a chance to enjoy both the big things, like the mountains, the river, and the ocean, and the little things, like the profusion of wild flowers and wild animals … and generally to savor life for a change."

"Like this lovely meal in this gorgeous setting," I continued. "I just wanted to say, though, how sorry I continue to be over Alex's death. I can't imagine how you have coped with his loss over the years."

A lengthy silence followed. Then, Dr. Peter spoke slowly and deliberately. "I'd be lying if I said we've never looked back. But we try not to, because if we do, we do no one any favors … not us, not you, not Simon. He doesn't need us to blame him — or his damned noise-maker — or you or ourselves for our decision to let Alex go on that ride."

He paused again for a moment before adding, "We just have to show Simon that the way for medical practitioners like us to live healthy and productive lives is to provide the best possible service to whatever community we end up in … and just take it from there."

"Thank you so much for saying that," I replied, with corresponding emphasis. "You have no idea how it helps me personally as well … and how much I look forward to seeing you both and Simon at my lodge."

As it turned out, 28-year-old Simon arrived at the lodge by himself the following Friday. He said his parents would have loved to have come, but were busy working.

He himself had booked off early, and was in a decidedly upbeat mood, wearing a casual khaki jacket, white shirt, and dark-brown chino pants. He looked tall, lean, and athletic with a shock of thick brown hair.

With a genuine smile on her face that I hadn't seen for a very long time, Jess boldly asked Simon whether he would like a ride on a very gentle horse. He paused, and then tentatively said yes. "Sure, I'll give it a go. It's about time I did."

So, she saddled up Chester, the most bulletproof of our horses, and spent some time familiarizing him with Simon … and vice versa.

When Simon was completely comfortable with the idea, she led both out on a gentle trail ride through a Shadow Mountain meadow. She didn't push either horse or rider, and made sure Chester and her own gelding stayed at a quiet, steady walk with little or nothing to scare them.

It was a beautiful evening as the sun went down like a blood-red sleeping bag … and everything, for a change, was just right.

Jess pointed out to Simon the various peaks and glaciers she had come to know and love. And she told me later she forgot all about the pain and built-up frustration in her life, adding that Simon was very different from either Joel or Matt.

"I've never had a man be so attentive," Jess said. "He was so easy to be with, and curious about everything from my views on horses and Maverick Valley politics to those on my own career future," she said. "He seemed really interested in what I had to say — which, for me, was a major change."

Jess added, "Our time together seems so effortless. But what I particularly like is how gentle he is with Chester."

Simon, who had a charming way of cocking his head and running his fingers through his hair, told me the ride was just what he needed. It was both a confidence booster following his brother's long-ago riding tragedy and a welcome break from his hospital work.

"I thought I'd never get back on a horse," he said. "But Jess is so calm and reassuring she's removed all doubt from my mind that I could do it. And I can."

My only question was whether Simon really was wowed by his time on the horse … or by the time spent with Jess, with whom he seemed to be already smitten. I could see genuine sparks between them, and I didn't believe it was wishful thinking.

Their age difference didn't appear to bother either of them. And it didn't concern me. When it came to love and harmony, age was just a number. But then I always have been a romantic.

CHAPTER 16

MADAM LUNA

Running an "ethical escort agency" in the Maverick Valley area, as maverick Madam Luna claimed to be doing in her colorful publicity blurb, was problematic from the start.

Your neighbors, tolerant though they might be of wolves howling or fireworks going off in the middle of the night, might think you were either a typical, tiresome feminist, or a hypocritical harlot.

I mean, what really is ethical about escorting? It's just the world's oldest profession wrapped up in a more wholesome-sounding name. Or at least that's what Luna's legion of critics argued.

But Hong-Kong-born Luna was clearly onto something. In these days of quickie divorces and prolonged gender divisions, having safe and ethical (or relatively safe and ethical) sex might seem better than no sex at all. And the more easygoing of the often-lonely eccentrics who lived in the valley — or the humming town of Homage itself — seemed to appreciate that fact.

Always expensively dressed, Luna was a divorced accountant who had discovered the hard way that husbands — and increasingly wives — occasionally strayed. And one relatively painless way to do this was to employ the "intimacy services" of professional "escorts" to avoid the exhausting and potentially marriage-ending complications of extramarital affairs.

She herself had been round a block or two. And she suspected that, if you set strict, safety-aware boundaries for both sex workers and clients, growth in the consumer-friendly business in a highly underserved area could be virtually limitless … especially in the era of AI. The key was efficiency, economy, and cross-promotion with related businesses.

Luna, in fact, was a staunch supporter of the proposed Maverick Valley mega resort which, despite stiff, vocal opposition, was poised to bring in thousands more cottagers and other potential customers to her Eden Escorts business: people looking for both indoor and outdoor adventure.

For example, drug-dealing Sandy, my former love interest, was part-owner of a night club frequented by young men and women in desperate need of money to finance their party lifestyle. And he was already her ally. In fact, he and Luna seemed joined at the career hip.

This realization had put the petite Luna, whose delicate jade earrings instantly caught my eye, firmly in my sights. After all, I was both Sandy's ex-partner, Jess's mother, and the official spokeswoman for the anti-development coalition.

So, when she phoned to ask me over for a quiet chat, I paid her a brief visit in the highly secure, waterfront penthouse where she resided with Bella, her white, fluffy Bichon Frise.

It was a suite with an eclectic mix of potted and hanging plants, ceramic vases, and pop art. Judging by her quality interior decorations, you could be forgiven for thinking she was a gallery owner rather than a brothel operator.

After mixing me a smoothie and pouring herself a gin and tonic, Luna sat me down on the shiny leather, living-room couch. And, at first, she denied having anything to do with support for the Maverick development proposal. Then, when faced with incontrovertible evidence to the contrary, she switched to saying she supported all — or virtually all — businesses in the Homage area.

"But I never want to have to pay homage to anyone in particular," she quipped.

"And I don't want to be constantly fighting and trading barbs with you," I replied, "though I have my doubts that your business is as feminist and pro-female as it's cracked up to be. Or as secure and safe."

"It's likely far better than the alternative, which is street prostitution, male pimping, and female degradation," she replied with refreshing candor. "In any case,

I'm thinking that as fellow forward-thinking businesswomen, you and I should be able to reach some kind of truce."

"A mutually beneficial one, I hope," I said, agreeing that we both needed to get off our respective high horses, take a large, deep breath, relax, and just talk.

"Well, Kyra, you took issue with the 'ethics' of my business in your recent humdinger of a valley anti-development speech. At least, I assume it was Eden you were talking about, not some other 'ethical' escort service I was unaware of."

"No, it was Eden. But I mentioned it only in passing. And I didn't think you would mind in the least. I mean, as P.T. Barnum once said, there's no such thing as bad publicity."

"I don't know about that. But I do think that, if you stop attacking my business and even start supporting it, I can help you keep tabs on people and things you may want to know more about."

"How so?" I asked.

"We have files, tapes, and photos of everything … or most things anyway. And that kind of knowledge is power of the kind you may need when, say, collecting bills, applying political pressure, or keeping tabs on wayward family members."

I didn't know the specifics of what she was saying. But Luna, who was dressed in a turquoise silk jacket and flowing pink pants, obviously kept herself well-informed. She was well-prepared to spring into swift, decisive action on any number of business fronts, coalitions, and conspiracies.

Besides, I could see clearly now that she could be either a powerful upstanding ally or a fierce, underhanded foe. And I vastly preferred the former to the latter.

So, for now, I chose to be her friend, if only a friend whom I could occasionally bounce some ideas off. Ethics, I'm afraid, had little to do with it.

French author Albert Camus once said that a man without ethics is a wild beast loosed upon this world. But Canadian author Maxime Lagacé noted, "What you think shows nothing. What you say shows little. What you do shows everything."

Yes, men and women should be judged for what they do, not what they pontificate about. I certainly didn't want to let my being a fuddy-duddy, self-martyring prig get in the way of my doing some good for my family and our besieged community. And we were under some heavy kind of siege, believe me.

Before getting up from the couch and making my way to the door, I realized again that Luna was really not an ally. She was a force I would have to watch carefully. But we parted cordially, agreeing to stay in touch.

CHAPTER 17

JACOB

Jacob was an enigma. As an aging Native American who reportedly drank too much, he always seemed to be carrying a great weight of sorrow on his shoulders … except when he was on horseback or helping another horse or rider. Then, you could feel the whole lightness of his being.

A former top bronc rider, he was one of several locals standing up for the group of wild horses accused by officials of endangering public safety by "terrorizing" motorists and causing dangerous collisions on the main valley road. He maintained the solution was simple.

"The highway people should just fence off the highway," Jacob was quoted in the local media as saying. "It's not the horses terrorizing the traffic, it's the traffic terrorizing them."

I liked Jacob for his bold stand on the flight-happy horse band. I mean, why can't motorists simply slow down and be a little more careful and watchful? They must know they're in a wildlife-rich area.

I also respected his deep overall equine knowledge. I remember him telling me how Native Americans trying to "break" wild horses used to take them to the river to mount … because they wouldn't buck in the water. It was a simple but effective schooling technique.

Above all, I believed him to be a fellow free spirit. Sure, we had vast differences in our respective upbringings. But he too seemed to understand that politics tends to drive people apart, while riding brings them together.

As he once told me, we all have to put our riding boots on one step at a time. And horses are great equalizers. They don't seem to be too impressed by human rank, privilege, or how much money you have in the bank.

Besides, I figured Jacob was just what my grieving daughter, Jess, needed at this trying time. Despite her wonderful ride with Simon, she was still reeling from boyfriend Matt's horrific death … and from ugly local chatter that had fingered her for his fall. After all, she was the one overheard by nearby mountain-bikers saying she wanted to kill him.

Also, Jess had come to mistrust her friend and workmate Joel, whom she felt was trying to take advantage of Matt's death by making moves on her. Joel had grown ever more controlling, and she said it felt at times as if he was "stalking" her. "I like his energy, but I've had it with domineering men."

Jess would still spend long hours in her lodge cabin doing who knows what, and only emerge when absolutely needed — even when I reminded her that Sheriff Luke was on the case and was certain he would get to the bottom of it.

One afternoon, I thought it was high time Jess and I stepped out of our respective boxes. And I asked her to go with me to the nursery in Homage to find some flowers for the deck area … where visitors would sit in front of the lodge, watch the horses graze, and drink coffee or sip local wine.

I wanted the deck to be a focal point for resting, reading, chatting, dreaming — and gazing.

The nursery — run by Lily, my super-organized neighbor — provided its usual super-service. And we proceeded to buy a collection of potted plants, including begonias, petunias, and primroses. We carefully loaded them into the back of the truck and drove home to pot them in the deck planters. They added a vital splash of vibrant color, which, I felt, served as a turning point. "That's a job well done," I told Jess. "I love the look we've created for this key area of the lodge."

Then, Jess and I eased into the deck's red Adirondack chairs to enjoy a cool evening drink of lemonade together.

The discussion turned to Simon and his parents. And I said I was impressed with how the family had rallied around each other following Alex's tragic death all those years ago … and had found their purpose in providing topnotch medical services to those in need of it. I also liked the way they hadn't blamed me for the tragedy, and instead had let us into their lives.

"Yes, Simon doesn't seem too scarred by it," Jess said, "though I don't think he's completely over it either. He says that, despite his great ride on Chester, he is still leery of horses after all these years. The logical side of his brain forgave him a long time ago, but the emotional side still hasn't."

"Talking of horses," I said. "Appy is looking good out there in the front pasture. And I think it's time we started to ride him in earnest. He's five now."

"Yes, I love that horse," Jess replied. "He's so gentle … and trainable."

"Well, let's train him," I said. "Or better still. Let's get Jacob to come over and help us do the schooling. People say Jacob's over the hill. But I think he's still the best there is in the valley. Besides, we'll learn so much other stuff from him."

Jacob didn't take much persuading to come over for a training session. We joined him on the newly refurbished deck for a coffee and fresh muffin. Lean and languid, he wore a battered straw cowboy hat and jeans with a shiny, bucking-bronco buckle. His shirt was light pink with pearl-snap fasteners. His eyes had stories to tell, and his voice was soft but firm. He moved quietly. I could see why horses liked him.

He said he loved Appaloosas, with their eye-catching, spotted coats and fugitive American Indian ancestry, though he noted they were prone to eye problems.

"The one thing I always say when breaking a horse: Be patient. Don't be in a hurry. You don't need to be. I mean the days when you suddenly have to pull up stakes and head for Canada — as the Nez Perce had to do — are long gone."

Jacob himself never seemed to be hurried. He had a way of walking shaped by years in the saddle. He would slowly and rhythmically lean from one side to the other, like a seasoned sailor on a storm-tossed ship.

Jess asked him what was the first thing that she needed to do to help Appy become more ridable.

"Your best first step is to build a relationship with the young horse," he said. "When you've done that — and it will take more time than you think — the rest is simple. Appy seems happy, approachable, and willing. If you click with him, Jess, he'll do anything for you."

Later, Jacob, Jess, and I sauntered down to the barn, reached for Appy's halter and caught up to him in the pasture. Then we brought him into the riding arena. And Jacob said, "Give me a few minutes, Jess, to start to get to know him."

Simon, whom Jess had invited to watch the proceedings from the arena's viewing benches suddenly appeared … and appeared mesmerized.

"My experiences with horses haven't always been good," he told Jess. "But I see now why you love them and why you want to be a vet."

"I see now why you wanted to be a doctor," she replied. "And you've done it, and I respect the sacrifices you've made to do it. I still have a long way to go to become a vet."

"If you love animals and getting there, it'll pass in no time," a smiling Simon replied, giving her a gentle hug, running his hand through his hair and tilting his head towards her.

They looked genuinely happy together. And Jacob later remarked that he himself now had a good feel for the horse. "Let's set up a time for our first training session. We'll take it slow, but we'll get you aboard Appy sooner than you think. You've got a good one here. A real keeper."

CHAPTER 18

THE DATE

The next day, I phoned Sheriff Luke to tell him how well things had gone with the Handsworths — and with Jess and Jacob. "We'll even have you riding here soon," I said.

"You mean you want me to race you bareback over a set of irrigation ditches in the sagebrush," Luke joked. "Well, to hell with that!"

I also told him of Jess's misgivings about Joel, but added that he remained a good worker and a guest favorite.

"Far be it for me to interfere," Luke said. "But if you like, I could talk to Joel and gently reinforce the fact that Jess needs time to heal by herself and doesn't need any more stress, especially from him."

"No, she does not," I repeated, both as a statement of fact and a warning from a fiercely protective mother.

"Well, I'll go see Joel and have another little sheriff-style chat with him," he added. "So far there's nothing tying him to Matt's death."

"Nothing at all?" I asked.

"No, nothing was found to indicate this was anything more than an accidental fall … or a possible suicide. Marijuana was found in his body. But the pathologist said there was nothing unusual about that."

"What about the mountain bikers in the vicinity at the time?"

"None of them have changed their story. They say what they heard was a loud argument followed by silence," Luke said. "You never know, though, in this kind of case. Someone will come forward with something at some point.

"Changing the subject, though, how are your political activities going?"

"Most people I talk to seem to agree with me that the proposed development is way over the top, though that doesn't mean too much," I said. "A lot of local businesspeople are struggling and see only the dollar signs. They will stay away from me and my campaign. But I did have an interesting chat with Madam Luna. She seems to be clued in about, well, everything that's going on."

"The business she's in gives her a bird's-eye view, so to speak," Luke laughed. "But what about you? How are you doing … personally, I mean? I heard about the breakup with Sandy, but are you and he still talking to each other?"

"Not really. I mean we talk, and he can be a charmer. But I just don't trust him anymore. I sense, as you do, that he's involved in the illegal drug business and in whatever nefarious activities are going on at the night club. So, I've warned Jess to stay away from there."

"Good. Keep her well away. Neither you nor I would want to see her face on the TV news. In the meantime, how about you and I going out some time?"

"You mean on a real date," I asked, a little flustered.

"Yes. But only if you promise not to bring up my horse-racing abilities."

"Those were the days, my friend," I sighed. "They were simpler, crazier and, I suspect, happier than now. I miss them."

"I'm not sure I do," Luke replied. "For some reason, I never really felt I fit in at that ranch. It was all a bit too much for me. Too many rich Easterners, I guess."

"You were a good guy, a hard worker, and a fine wrangler. But talking of ranch work, how's your father, is he still in good health?"

"Yes, but the more he says he wants to be independent, the more he seems to need my help around the place. Is your mom hanging in okay?"

"Thanks for asking. She still seems stunned by Dad's death and the move to the care home. And you and I are both at the age when we have to help out that generation quite a bit. But enough of the small talk, I'd better get to work. Let me know when you want to pick me up … for the date, I mean. I'm looking forward to it."

"I've been looking forward to it for years," he said, touching my shoulder lightly.

The date at the Waterview Grill went well, given all the drama surrounding it. In fact, you could say it went far better than I expected. I was starting to get to know the eating place ... and they me.

Looking out at the swirling river as it poured its way into the glacier-fed, turquoise ocean framed the evening perfectly. Plus, the seafood and steak portions were filling, if not exactly thrilling. I even had a chocolate dessert … though food was really the last thing on my mind.

Luke looked a little different — less like an uptight cop and more like a man about town. He'd obviously taken some Internet tips about how men can look dapper and put their best foot forward. But my conclusion was the same. With Luke, you knew where you stood. Then and now. He showed up on time. He did what he said he was going to do. And I had to pinch myself that I was getting a second crack at him.

The fact is most people don't really change that much, although they may develop better table manners.

So, Luke could mend a fence, fix a tire, catch a crook, and patch a relationship. But could he sweep one off one's feet? Or did that not matter so much at my stage of life?

At least he seemed to have progressed from the shy, young wrangler of old into a man who was comfortable in his own skin, and confident to boot. He looked good, too.

One major issue, at least for me and my sanity, was his job. He was always being beeped at all hours of the night and day. And, as a habitually hands-on boss, he had to respond … or felt he had to.

So, I was not surprised when Murphy's Law applied and a "pressing" emergency call abruptly cut short our mutual-admiration session.

Luke responded as if shot by a cannon. And I realized that, if our budding relationship were to bloom, I'd have to get used to sudden exits as well as delayed entrances … and a few crazy bareback rides.

In fact, I'd have to get used to a lot of things, including feeling safe, secure, and sincere about a man for a change … and being able possibly to plan a life together. Now, that thought excited me.

CHAPTER 19

JEALOUSY

"Joel," I shouted as he headed out of the barn in the morning. "Did you see the bear?"

"No," he replied without enthusiasm, as if trying to figure out why anyone would be interested in black bear sightings that were a daily occurrence in the valley, especially during blackberry season.

"Well, a bear seems to have got the horses racing around the pasture," I said. "And Belle's front left shoe looks as if it's about to come off. Would you mind taking a look?"

"Okay, I'll see to it," he replied, heading back to the cubbyhole in the barn where he slept when he wasn't staying at his father's place. It was where he kept the farrier's tools he'd cadged from Sandy, including everything from an anvil to hoof knives, rasps, clinches, hammers, and nippers. He stowed them away in an old blacksmith's box, along with a set of unshaped horseshoes.

Joel may not have been the most patient person when it came to horses. And he certainly wasn't the kindest. But he still prided himself on the shoeing skills he'd inherited from Sandy and his Irish grandfather. He was truly a handy man.

Using a carrot as a bribe, Joel caught the large roan mare, brought her into the barn, put her in a stall, removed both front shoes, and trimmed her hooves. He did it as smoothly, easily, and swiftly as if he were a manicurist giving a regular client a professional nail job.

Belle would now run around barefoot.

But that didn't bother me, as I wasn't ready to let Joel or Jess rent out any of the horses yet for rides on the rocky trails. I had to be absolutely certain the ponies wouldn't spook, act up, or run away with someone. That prospect still held too many bad memories.

As for the barn, both Joel and Jess kept it in good nick. It was their work space and was, in fact, in better shape than the main lodge … which had all the character in the world, but was crying out for attention.

The living room had beat-up, crinkly leather chairs, musty lighting, a river-rock fireplace that leaked smoke, and a wobbly, uneven dining table. The floor badly needed re-sanding and the roof fixing. It was lovable, but still not entirely livable.

The lodge, though, had a couple of major things going for it. It had a great deck and mountain views to die for. And it was situated close enough to the river for you to be able to see and feel its mighty rush, while also being high enough above it to be able to withstand the heaviest of flooding.

Flooding, if the truth be known, was a far worse menace in the valley than either berry-mad bears, semi-wild horses, or cash-hungry escorts.

The most recent flood happened just the other day along the forest service road, a winding dirt thoroughfare beloved of hikers and campers that began where the paved road ended. That washout brought traffic to a halt for several hours. And I mean all traffic, because there wasn't an alternate route.

A major valley flood, however, could ruin your whole day, week, or the better part of the month. And that's when valley residents would begin stopping by my lodge, viewing it both as a refuge and a source of information.

There was always some dry spot on my land … and someone here willing to try to explain to them what they'd have to do if they couldn't make it back into their own flood-encircled home.

I liked it that way. In fact, my vision for the lodge had always taken this into consideration. Sure, I wished for a place where out-of-towners could sample fresh, homegrown food while staying in a historic-looking farmhouse … and where their children could play in a forest wonderland or fuss over the rabbits, goats, and other animals. I even looked forward to hosting the odd business conference or wedding.

But what I never wanted to lose sight of was the notion of "welcome" that my parents, with all their failings, once offered. I wanted Shadow Mountain Lodge to be a welcoming place. As author Shauna Niequist said, "the heart of hospitality is about creating space for someone to feel seen and heard and loved."

Now at some point, of course, Joel must have felt that way about the lodge. He likely thought of it a haven of sociability, togetherness — and possibly even hot dates — in a valley relatively remote from hip urban civilization. He certainly appeared to do so.

But as my relationship with his father sputtered and died, and his hoped-for liaison with Jess failed to take off, he clearly started to view things differently.

One moment, Joel was firmly on board with my mission to turn Shadow Mountain Lodge into a legendary, warm-and-friendly, close-to-nature spread, similar to the hyper-social Aspen Ranch where I once worked as a kid wrangler. The next, he was sneering at the guests, shadowing Jess, and even challenging my right to boss him. It was also a little unclear exactly what he was doing when he was in the barn, or what secrets he might be hiding.

It all came to a head one afternoon when Jess asked Simon to view one of Jacob's now regular training sessions with Appy … and invited him to stay for dinner.

Soon after Simon arrived and became visibly affectionate with Jess, Joel made a loud, snarky comment about "everything smelling around here." He said Jacob smelled of drink and Simon of high-powered antiseptic.

Jess was appalled, but let it drop … until Joel proceeded to needle Simon more directly, accusing him of cradle-snatching, and eventually even challenging him to a fist fight.

Simon responded by asking Joel whether he was high on something and, if he was, suggested he might be better off lying down and sleeping it off.

Joel erupted, yelling at Jess and fingering Simon as he stormed off, frightening both me and the horses. Jacob stated simply, "There's a young man with an old problem. Jealousy."

CHAPTER 20

LUKE

Luke showed up at the lodge, as promised, to caution Joel about his pestering of Jess and his bothering of Simon. But the real reason Luke came, I sensed, was to open up to me about, well, many things both past and present.

Over a cup of joe, he told me how his roots were still in the valley on his dying father's ranch, but that he'd gone from job to job in his police career until he wound up as a homicide detective on Seattle's mean streets.

Sadly, that experience shattered his opinion of the world as a fundamentally benevolent, honest place — and replaced it with it being a cesspit of corruption and insidious, endlessly divisive politics.

"Truth," he said, "is not only the first casualty of war, but of policing."

"I think that's the case with a lot of jobs," I said, "especially those where you're dealing directly with the public. Even here at the lodge, I run into politics. I mean, look at my campaign against the planned Maverick monstrosity. Many of my friends have already accused me of having morphed into a political animal — or at least into someone or something they can't fully trust."

"Yes, I suppose you're right," Luke replied. "It's just that so often the police are made out by the media to be paragons of virtue, when they're not. Far from it. We're just struggling to stay alive and keep our heads above water and avoid the worst of the heavy flooding."

"But without police, what a lawless bunch we'd be," I countered. "Someone has to do the job. And you're obviously good at it. They like you in the valley. And they're a funny lot, especially when it comes to authority figures they're forced to finance through their taxes. Then, they seem to care more about the state of the bears and other local wildlife than about the humans living around here."

"Talking of which," Luke added, "I hear from the wildlife authorities that a mountain lion and three kittens have been sighted in your area. They seem to be losing their fear of humans … just like the human cougars."

"So, do you really think I'm a cougar?"

"No, just a wild thing, one that makes my heart sing," Luke replied, finally loosening up.

Just then, Joel pedaled back into the lodge with his first group of mountain-bikers of the day. He looked happy, confident, and relaxed, especially while pocketing their tips.

But, unlike the appreciative guests, I wasn't fooled by his increasingly Jekyll and Hyde character. Nor was Luke, who wasted no time in sitting him down and quizzing him about his recent bad-boy behavior. He also asked him to explain exactly where he was when Matt fell to his death.

"I've told you once, and I'll tell you again. I was in the barn, where I always am when I'm not out on the mountain," Joel said defiantly.

"Okay, don't be so touchy, Joel," Luke ordered. "I'm trying to get to the bottom of this. I mean it's weird that Matt, who flies down mountains for a living, would allow himself to tumble to his death off a mountain while on a relaxing, supposedly stress-free holiday."

"Well, go ask Jess," Joel said. "She's the one who was climbing with him and was heard getting into a shouting match with him. She's the one with the really lousy temper, not me. Matt probably just got royally pissed off with her and decided to get stoned. Falling off a cliff might have seemed like a major relief."

Luke ignored that crass, insensitive remark, clearly realizing the interview with Joel was going nowhere. Instead, he accepted my invitation to stay for a soup-and-sandwich lunch.

This gave me a chance to detail some of the many problems I'd had in my marriage with Rory and my later relationship with Sandy. I did this so that Luke would know my life, too, hadn't been a bed of roses.

I pointed out that Jess had also suffered … and perhaps more than me. Which was why I was so glad she had finally found a man with dreamy brown eyes like Simon.

"Do you really think he's a keeper?" Luke asked. "I mean, are you now hearing wedding bells?"

"The sooner the better," I replied. "They seem to be on some kind of mission to save the world — with her as a vet for the animals and him a doctor for the humans. I like that."

"His parents seem like good, caring people, too," Luke added. "Or at least they're not the kind to duck out when the going gets tough and the public's screaming blue murder. They're always a great help and support to us in the department."

Afterwards, we walked down to the bank of the heaving, swollen river, murky with glacial discharge and unspoken deadly menace. Luke held my hand and said, "I know I don't say this often enough, but whenever I'm with you, you manage to make me smile."

"You make me smile, too," I replied. "And I never realized, until now, all that you've gone through in your life. You always seem so cool, calm, and collected. You fix things. You calm them. You don't stir them up. That's why mavericks like Madam Luna like you."

"Not really, I just conceal my worries better than some," said Luke playfully. "The fact is I'm quite a shy, nervous, and excitable person. In fact, when I'm around you, my pulse is always racing."

That warm, light-hearted admission was just what I needed, given all that was going on. It made me feel much closer to him. And no, no cougars were in view. But a bald eagle soared overhead. And as we hugged for the first time of any significance, I thought I saw a slice of heaven, shimmering with shafts of sunlight.

CHAPTER 21

JOEL

Still smarting from his exchange with Luke, Joel headed to town for a happy pill — or two. Then, he went to the hospital to hang out and see if he could "accidentally" run into Simon.

From what I pieced together later, Joel wanted to let the good doctor know he didn't think he was "a good fit" for Jess, a young woman who needed someone who wasn't "so dull and stuffy."

"She's an outdoor girl and loves her freedom," Joel apparently told Simon. "She's much too much of a woman for you. Besides, she has a temper you won't like when you really get to know her."

Simon revealed to me he tried reasoning with Joel in the reception area, but to no effect. "He was very agitated and on edge," he said, adding he had to call security when matters escalated and the confrontation started to get "irrational and physical."

Eventually, a couple of large, laidback security officers arrived and shepherded the jazzed-up Joel out into the lot where he'd parked his Ford Mustang. They told him to "just go home and chill."

Instead, Joel lingered in the lot, waiting for Simon, who had been called out to visit an elderly patient living up the valley.

Simon said that, as he eased out onto the road in his late-model Subaru WRX, Joel snuck into the traffic behind him, but kept his distance. He no doubt feared the full-throated roar of the Mustang's hot V-8 engine might tip Simon off that he was being followed. Or maybe at this point he didn't care.

Simon had phoned me to say he was thinking of stopping by the lodge to see Jess, as he hoped to take her with him on his home visit. He explained it was beautiful on the forest service road, and thought they might enjoy an evening walk there together before heading back to Homage for a fish-and-chip supper.

I replied that Jess was now out on the trails with a group of mountain-bikers, which was why she couldn't be reached by cellphone. I added that she was actually filling in for Joel, who had booked off sick for the afternoon. And I figured she wouldn't be back for at least an hour.

"Well, Joel may be sick," Simon said, "but not in the way you might expect. He was actually in Homage hospital just now causing a ruckus, and I had to have him removed."

"I'm really sorry, Simon, that you had to go through that. Maybe it's finally time I let him go."

"Don't do it just because of me," he replied. "I think I can handle him. But what he really needs is psychological help. In any case, let's discuss it later. Meanwhile, please let Jess know I'm on my way and will try to phone her when I've finished my house call. Thanks again for all your help."

What was clear from this conversation was that Joel was literally going round the bend. However, Jess and Simon were spending more and more time together, and had become inseparable.

For now, Joel kept his distance behind Simon. But as they motored further up the road, the doctor looked in his mirror and saw the Mustang coming up fast behind him, being driven erratically. He said he was convinced Joel was either on something or suffering from a bad case of road rage … and meant to chase him down one way or another.

Both drivers were speeding on a two-lane, winding road that was flanked by dense forest and offered limited visibility. It was where the drivers of logging trucks and other heavy equipment often held up impatient motorists, causing a lot of shouting, fist-shaking, and horn-honking.

The more powerful Mustang clearly had the better straight-line speed, while the all-wheel-drive Subaru was quicker and more stable in the corners. And as the paved road ended and the bumpy service road began, the gap between Simon and Joel widened.

The speed at which the men drove was still frightening … or at least it must have seemed that way to the herd of mustangs ahead, darting across the road in a cloud of dust.

Panic seized the feral animals as Simon, with Joel on his tail, appeared set to barrel into them.

"It was a white-knuckle ride," Simon said. "I thought I was done for. I mean, there was a sheer cliff to the left and a steep uphill slope to the right, with the panicked horses zig-zagging in between at full gallop."

He added, "I barely had time to brake and only just missed hitting one or more of them."

The young doctor said it was clear his mad pursuer didn't have time to stop. Or perhaps he didn't even try to. Instead, Joel veered violently from the right to the left of the roadway with his tires screeching and skidding on the loose gravel … and plunged over the edge.

"And that's why they call it Devil's Cliff," said Simon, who stopped abruptly and leapt out of his car. In disbelief, he watched as the Mustang plummeted over the precipice, cartwheeling down end-over-end and leaving a trail of flying metal and glass.

Finally, it smashed into the rock-hard slope with a sickening thud. An eerie moment of silence followed. Then, the Mustang exploded in a fireball, likely killing Joel instantly.

Simon told me he couldn't believe what had just happened. He had come to Homage for a quiet, quasi-rural life. And here he was witnessing the death of a deranged young man who was out to murder him — and who might have done so, but for serendipity and the wild horses.

Stunned, Simon said he went white with shock, his heart pounding from adrenalin, and his hands shaking like a leaf. He paused for a while, pacing about, and looking down to check there was no sound of life coming from the wreck below him.

Then, he returned to his Subaru, jumped in and slowly turned the car around — and drove it back to find cell service. He made several calls, trying his level best to remain calm, collected, and in his emergency-doctor mode.

When the search-and-rescue crew members finally arrived, they had to use ropes to remove Joel's lifeless, badly burned body and hoist it — and what was left of the battered car — up onto the roadway. The horses by then had long vanished.

Joel's funeral at the Homage Funeral Chapel was a muted affair, with a few friends and family members present. Jess, Simon, Luke, and I attended out of a sense of duty to the community. Any death in the valley, however it came about, affected everyone and deserved recognition. In life and death, I believed we should all stick together.

I agreed with Luke, though, that Joel was a deeply troubled young man on a self-destructive path. He had got what was coming to him. Given his level of jealousy, he was either destined to wind up dead or kill or maim some other love rival.

Sandy was at the chapel, too, looking somber in a dark suit. But seized, no doubt, with profound grief at the tragic loss of his son, he kept to himself. He wasn't interested in talking.

He did take time, though, to give me a comforting touch on the shoulder, and thanked Jess and me for coming. We hugged warmly for what might have been, had fate only dealt us all a different set of cards.

Jess herself had very mixed emotions. She had known Joel was jealous of both Matt and Simon. She also knew that some men became highly possessive when they set their sights on a female whom they found particularly appealing.

But Joel's behavior had been beyond controlling. It was psychotic. He was clearly a man of extremes. And his hounding of Jess and stalking of Simon suggested someone who had severe mental problems … even though career-wise he appeared to have a lot going for him.

Jess reiterated that, until recently, she had considered Joel to be a capable work companion and a mostly helpful friend. But after hearing in greater detail how the "accident" occurred, with Joel recklessly pursuing Simon, her ultimate reaction was one of relief.

Joel, Jess said, must have known that engaging in what amounted to a high-speed duel on such a treacherous road could well prove fatal to either of the men. It was both suicidal and homicidal.

But she was well and truly glad it was Simon who survived. Her burgeoning relationship with the man whom she now said she loved the most in her stormy young life could proceed without turbulence … or at least on the straight and narrow.

CHAPTER 22

BUSINESS

When I was making my living as a photographer, I was preoccupied with the element of surprise, both when taking a picture and while presenting it to viewers in a way that might hold their interest.

That's perhaps why I like what I'm doing now … because running a lodge, especially one that's off the beaten track, is almost always a surprise. One day is rarely like another.

So, I was really not that surprised to receive a phone call out of the blue from Seattle business dynamo Ali Thomas, even though the last time we had chatted was, oh, a decade ago.

I had shot a series of feature pictures of her for *Lakeside Magazine*, a glossy publication specializing in high-end, country retreats.

That was shortly after she had started a company specializing in hiring female techies to contract positions with major corporations. To everyone's surprise except

Ali's, that company, SheTech Solutions, took off like a rocket. And Ali later sold most of it, only to branch out into land-heavy real estate and small hotels designed for eco-minded, outdoorsy people.

She'd invested at just the right time, and now was worth millions.

I recognized her cheerful, energetic voice right away. "I'll be up in your neck of the woods next Tuesday, and would absolutely love to take you out for coffee … so we can have a catch-up chat. That is if you're not too busy."

"I'm never too busy to talk to Seattle's businesswoman of the year," I flattered in true business-like fashion.

"Well, I'd just like to pick your brains about something. Discretely. How about Elspeth's Corner at 10:30 a.m.?"

"Yes, that would be fine," I said. "It's a good place to meet and be discreet."

Elspeth's Corner was a funky, neo-Victorian café sandwiched between one end of Maverick Valley and the beginning of Homage town. It served everything: from goat milk and cheese for people allergic to cow's milk, homegrown honey, and one-of-a-kind, home-baked treats. And, of course, great coffee.

Elspeth herself lived on a small acreage just down the road from my lodge, with a dozen sheep for wool (for both spinning and dyeing) and several goats, who were elite escape artists in the high Houdini manner.

With auburn hair, green eyes, and freckles, Elspeth had a smile that would light up an art gallery. And with two university-age sons and husband Rick, a retired stuntman, she wore the pants in her family … with colorful skirts, earth-toned cardigans, and practical but on-trend boots.

Underneath the granola trappings, though, Elspeth was all business. The bottom line was tops with her. And she definitely had a flair for hiring people of character at her café. "Maverick Valley folks like their servers to come with the flavor to match whatever it is they're serving," she explained.

"Look over there. That girl with the crewcut, the tattoos and the orange-and-light-green hair is Rosy. I've just hired her. She's from the valley, and she's dressed to turn heads, not just blend in with the furniture. Oh, and she's smart as a whip as a writer."

Ali arrived right on time, as expected. Lean and statuesque, she moved fluidly and looked classy yet understated in a navy-blue pantsuit and cream-colored satin shirt. She had delicate, double-hooped, copper earrings. But then Ali always liked to add flair with eye-catching jewelry. That was her hallmark.

After being handed a couple of medium-roast coffees by the artsy Rosy, we got straight down to business.

"Oh my god, those tattoos are not going to look so great when she's older," winked Ali, never one to skirt unpleasant truths.

"Yes, tattoos seem to be addictive. Rather like Kenya coffee. But at least they sometimes have a story to tell."

"I see you haven't lost your fine diplomatic touch," Ali said. "I guess you need it when dealing with the suits promoting that disastrous Maverick Valley megaproject."

"So, you think it's awful?"

"Yes, I think it is awfully ugly and completely out of step — and out of scale — with the community they're trying to force it on."

"It's refreshing to hear that from someone in the development industry," I said.

"I may be a developer, but I'm not a predator," Ali said. "I think selling real estate is like selling coffee: you give them what they want, not what you think they might want if they thought like you, hunched over in your high-rise office … the one with your MBA tattooed to the wall."

"I totally agree. But what can I do for you? Or you for me?" I asked directly.

"Well, let's make a deal. I will support your campaign against that monster development, if you will support me in my proposal for one of my boutique hotels on, or just off, this river. We already have the land lined up."

"Please go on, I am interested," I said.

"What I can assure you is we will make every effort to make the project fit in with the community. The customers we'll be targeting will be well-to-do, but down-to-earth folks with a passion for everything from river-rafting to horse-riding and biking to climbing.

And they will be providing loads of employment to the locals."

"But won't I simply be helping boost the competition and killing my own business? I mean, my lodge is geared to serving much the same outdoor-minded people."

"I think there is more than enough business — and future business — here for both of us. We would both benefit in many ways. In fact, I have considered making you an offer you can't refuse for your lodge. In any case, let's work together on this. It really is exciting."

"Yes, it certainly sounds so," I said. "There's no doubt that we do need employment for people like my daughter, Jess, and Elspeth's two sons who currently face a bleak work future in the valley. Not all the young ones here want to be forced to choose between heading off to the big city or remaining here penniless and dependent on their families."

"I'm really glad to hear you being so open-minded about this," Ali said. "Development in the valley is clearly growing, not slowing. And people here, however independent-minded, do need to have better jobs, homes, and health and education services, just like everyone everywhere. I mean they call it Maverick Valley, not Masochist Alley."

And with that bon mot, Ali and I became partners-in-arms. It was just a matter of working out a few nagging details … like how I was going to present her practical valley proposal to my anti-megaproject supporters without sounding like a complete hypocrite.

Ali seemed to think that could be worked out … remotely. But then she always was an optimist.

To celebrate our *entente cordiale*, I pulled out my iPhone and took a picture of her holding a jar of honey and looking genuinely delighted. I was pleasantly surprised at how well the shot turned out.

CHAPTER 23

SLOW WALTZ

If Ali's phone call was a bolt from the blue, the call from Martin Sterling, of Peregrine Holdings, was a rude awakening. Had he been spying on me and somehow listening in on my chit-chat with Ali at Elspeth's? Or was he just toying with me because he wanted to know more about my political ambitions and how they might affect his megaproject?

He was a tall, good-looking, stylish, and obviously wealthy man … or, as my bestie Carrie put it, "a fine piece of eye candy in his prime." And who says you should never mix pleasure with business?

So, despite my reservations about being in a conflict of interest, I agreed to meet him for a dinner meeting at the Waterview. Which was why I had to cut short my regular afternoon get-together with Carrie. I needed time to put on that little black dress.

"I must say, Carrie, I feel a little guilty about dancing with the devil, so to speak … both from a business and a personal point of view."

"You know your problem? You can never just go and have fun," she said. "I mean, if he was ugly and otherwise awful, would it be okay for you to go out with him then? Besides, you don't have to sleep with him. You can just feel him out!"

"I just feel I'm somehow letting Luke down," I sighed.

"Luke lets himself down," she replied. "He's always the cop on call. He's so regular he's a metronome. He should step out of his career box a bit, at least if he wants to corral you. You're a beautiful, energetic woman who wants and needs to let her hair down. I do, and it's the perfect tonic for working in a bank."

"What do you mean by 'letting my hair down'? I just had it cut!"

"I mean you should date a few more men, so you have something to compare Luke with," she said. "I know you're looking for someone reliable. But he must also be desirable — or at least sufficiently sure of himself to show he really desires you."

"Yes, I know that, Carrie."

"Or are you really just looking for a chief bottle-washer, caretaker, wrangler, and security person to keep your lodge running?"

It was a fair question, and one I had been asking myself a lot recently. Clearly, Carrie had picked up on it.

But the fact was that, like most women of my age, I had been pulled hither and thither for so long I didn't know which way was up.

Was I looking for a good time or a long time? Was I after deep caring and companionship or fleeting romantic love? Could I have it all?

I put on the black dress and a few other weapons suitable for close combat, and arrived fashionably late for my dinner date, er, meeting with Martin.

He was, as I had expected, looking in fine fettle. His manners were impeccable, which always puts an uneasy woman at ease. And there was just a hint of a twinkle in his eye, which also helps. In fact, I felt for the first time in ages I could let my hair down that night.

"Let's just forget for a moment what we don't have in common and focus on what we do," Martin suggested.

"That suits me fine. You are never going to persuade me to support your blessed project. So, it's probably best that you don't try. I mean, why spoil a lovely evening?"

"Why indeed? So why don't we just stick to discussing your political ambitions? I mean, are you planning to run for president in the fall and looking for hard cash?"

I laughed, as I usually do when I sense that a man sitting opposite me has a healthy sense of humor and is confident enough to try it out.

"Well, no, vice-president will do just fine. I'm a solid number-two person, just waiting to put my stamp on life in America and pad my investments. Talking of which, what are your politics?"

"I don't have any. I have the Peregrine mindset. I like to make money for myself and others … and have fun doing so. "As my old pappy used to say," he said, quoting TV character Bret Maverick, "a man does what he has to do — if he can't get out of it."

The conversation bubbled along, if not like champagne, at least like a fizzy energy drink on a sweltering day. I was having fun, too. We even had coffee afterwards — and a dance or two.

But then, just as I was doing a slow waltz with Martin, who should burst through the door? Well, Luke, of course. And he looked as if he had seen a ghost or drawn the wrong straw in a game of Russian roulette.

"Luke, what are you doing here?" I asked, breaking free from the firm clutches of the Peregrine man.

"I'm on sheriff's business," Luke exclaimed loudly, "and I'm having to check on what kind of riff-raff they're letting into this restaurant these days."

"He's not riff-raff," I said, lamely. "He's the man fronting the proposed megaproject. And we're having a serious discussion about the issues."

"Serious, my ass," the sheriff replied. "You're feeling each other up."

To say that the date with Martin, if it really was one, didn't end well would be an understatement. The two men squared off in the restaurant like pit bulls … large, square-jawed canines who were so enraged they didn't really know what they were angry about. Measured retreat was clearly not an option.

Bouncers were summoned, and it was a miracle that both my admirers weren't thrown out, which wouldn't have done Luke's reputation much good … or Martin's, for that matter.

I hastily — and sneakily — ordered a taxi and vowed never again to listen to Carrie's advice about dating in general and, in particular, about Luke being a boring, career-obsessed Goody Two-shoes. The man obviously had more passion than either Carrie or I had thought. Or at least he was more than ready to go to the mat for me. I liked that.

CHAPTER 24

UNFORGETTABLE

The next morning, I paced around the lodge with a cup of home-brewed coffee, feeling bad about what had transpired between Luke and Martin. Why, I asked myself, had I been so silly as to heed Carrie's suggestion about playing the field and Luke not being exciting enough for me?

Much as I loved Carrie, her unremitting friendship and her, well, maverick way of viewing life, she wasn't me. She worked at a bank with regular hours and staff-friendly lending rates, and had never been married to a charismatic, chronically selfish male abuser. She had also never had a child.

Luke and I had history together. He understood instinctively what I'd had to go through for all those years. And although he didn't find it easy to make his feelings known, I knew deep down he cared for me. And I cared about him.

He was protective and helpful without being super needy or otherwise suffocating. And I could see and feel that, or should have done so.

Luke also seemed to care about wanting to help Jess avoid the pitfalls presented by some of the more doubtful males in and around Maverick Valley and Homage. He warned me about her vulnerability. And that resonated with me, because Jess had recently told me to prepare for her settling down and marrying Simon — and putting all the destructive drama behind her. She said she was happy, determined, and in love.

As for Martin, of course it was nice to feel that a confident, attractive, powerful man like him would be interested in me. But I had to give my head a shake and remind myself he was simply using me to help Peregrine force its massive residential development onto the Maverick community. He wasn't pursuing me because he wanted a real relationship.

What a fool I'd been! I should have known better. Much better. Sometimes friends like Carrie, much as you think they might be trying to help you, can give you the worst advice. After all, no one really knows you better than you do yourself.

I dressed hurriedly and prepared to tackle everything on the lodge schedule for the day: from a new influx of exuberant visitors to a major construction upgrade planned for the lodge's main floor and a few of the guest cabins. I also felt it was high time I talked to Chelsea about worming the horses.

But what I was really thinking about was how I would soothe and otherwise handle Luke when we met … without losing him for good and all. Then, as if on cue, I looked outside the front window and saw his truck growling up the driveway.

He rapped on the door in a particularly insistent, cop-like way. I opened the door gingerly to see what his mood might be. Was he still angry about Martin? Had he decided to move back to Seattle? But without missing a beat, he took hold of me, moved in close, and gave me the fiercest of kisses. I felt his firm, warm embrace, his manly smell, and undeniable passion.

That is what I had been waiting for. And there it was, the truck-load of unblemished, unabashed affection I had needed and wanted for so long.

Our embrace seemed to last for an eternity until he softly let go, looked into my eyes, and said, "I love you with all my heart. I have ached for you for so long and I am not letting you go this time."

I breathed a deep sigh of relief and felt the longing I, too, had suppressed well up inside me. The guilt and shame rolled off me like mist from the mountains. I felt alive again.

Then, Luke and I sat down at the kitchen table and I made us both a fresh cup of coffee, the great peacemaker. And he opened up to me about himself … and about how his mother died when he was six in a car accident and how his father, who took to drink before developing early-onset Alzheimer's, still lived on the large family ranch far up the valley.

Luke added he himself sometimes stayed at the ranch, especially if he felt his dad's nervous nurse needed additional help. Most often, he still lived in his new-build condo in Homage, as it was so much more convenient for him. Also, it meant he could cover off most police-related events.

Then he confessed, in a way that made it seem as if he was laying all his cards on the table, there was a history of Alzheimer's in his family.

He recalled how his father, Jim, had started to forget key things at a fairly early age, and had had trouble solving basic problems. For example, he was unable to remember people's names and would lose track of the date or time of year. It made Christmas and birthdays particularly troublesome.

Later, Jim suffered from mood swings ... and became repetitious and suspicious about friends, family, and even his regular caregivers. "Now he has trouble speaking, feeding himself, and even swallowing," Luke said.

Listening to Luke, I could see how his mother's tragic death and the other hardships his family had faced had made him the shy, introspective and, yes, sensitive man he clearly was. And I felt terribly sad for him ... and for how I had failed to "read" him the way I should have.

I realized that, if only I'd been more aware of what he was going through, I would have treated him in a far less cavalier and superficial way than I had. Now I knew that, when he seemed wooden and apparently devoid of emotion, he was simply being true to himself.

I also knew the obstacles I'd be facing if I were, in fact, to marry him. And they didn't seem unsurmountable. They seemed like something we were in a relatively good position to tackle together.

And Carrie would just have to grow to like him.

CHAPTER 25

CHAPEL

The more each of us got to know the other, the more the approaching weddings of Luke and me — and, yes, Jess and Simon — were starting to seem like a contest over who would be first to tie the knot and where.

Luke and I decided to marry at the lodge, for the obvious reason that it was soon to be our joint home. Besides, we couldn't think of a friendlier, happier place for both humans and animals to hold a wedding. The welcome mat was never clearer or more obvious.

But we then figured we needed more time to get the lodge and the grounds ready for the kind of lively, Maverick-style get-together we wanted. Informality, I have found, often takes serious thought and planning.

Jess and Simon, meanwhile, opted for an earlier ceremony at St. Paul's Episcopal Church, a small log chapel situated right beside the Aspen Ranch where Luke and I worked years ago — and where Simon's seven-year-old brother, Alex, had died after that trail-ride fall and was buried.

We all agreed on one thing: Prior to Jess and Simon's wedding, we would all get together for a day to revisit the old ranch. After all, it was now part of National Park System. And we would get a close-up view of the graveyard where Alex was buried against a backdrop of jagged peaks in one of the most scenic parts of the world.

As Ansel Adams said, "No matter how sophisticated you may be, a large granite mountain cannot be denied — it speaks in silence to the very core of your being."

And, no, we wouldn't let guilt or any debilitating emotion play a huge part in it. Both for me, Luke, Jess and Simon, going back there was just a way of moving forward in our lives, as well as familiarizing Jess and Simon with their chosen wedding venue.

Luke drove us over in his crew cab, and we bonded and banded together without fuss or argument. There were some loose ends to be tied up, of course. But that was largely because the memory of Matt, the homicidal rage of Joel, and the politics of Maverick Valley were still raw.

That was life. Beauty is rarely pure and unalloyed, and love is never without patches of imperfection. As an unnamed cowboy poet once said,

There is no such thing as pure perfection.

All we can do is to try our best in the best of all possible worlds, and stop forever beating our chest.

In other words, you do the best you can with the cards you're dealt. You shuffle them one way and then another and trust that magic happens — as it so often does when wedding bells ring.

The Aspen Ranch was much as I remembered it, from the old Dutch barn where a pack horse once kicked me in the leg — and I received my first kiss from a cowboy — to the main lodge, wranglers' cabins, and dining building for the dudes.

Right there, in the shelter of a towering, snow-tipped peak, was the pasture where Luke once raced full tilt across those irrigation ditches. Shortly after, I stupidly let him out of my clutches. Not this time.

Armed with a packed lunch, we all hiked to the famed Emerald Lake Lookout, popular with hikers, back-packers, and climbers. Then we trudged on up a steep winding trail to the ranger station in the canyon where a group of late nineteenth-century explorers mysteriously went missing. We were exhausted and energized at the same time.

I have to say, though, that the old ranch atmosphere was absent. Missing were the shouts, curses, and guffaws of those long-ago days when the place was a thriving operation geared to well-heeled dudes and their families looking for a cool, summertime respite from the sizzling big city.

In those days, the ranch buzzed with action, adventure, and the knowledge that, once the brief summer was over and the fall hunting season done, you'd head down the road knowing you'd earned little, but learned a lot.

You'd also met fascinating people — from the canniest of city slickers to the heaviest-partying cowboys — whom you might, or might not, run into the following year for a further round of free-wheeling fun.

Still lurking there, though, were hazy memories of evening cookouts and dawn roundups of horses grazing overnight on the slopes … and of mist rising from the valley floor where the river twinkled, the moose wallowed, and the elk still roamed. It truly was a special place.

The chapel, built in the 1920s, offered much the same spectacular views, the same log construction, and the same tingling feeling that you were in another era … in which a handshake mattered and a person's word was his or her bond. So did their ability to ride a horse and look after themselves on the scariest of remote mountain trails.

The church itself could seat only about 60 people. But Jess and Simon were looking for a quiet, intimate wedding, as they both said they'd had enough noise and bustle in their everyday lives already.

They sought quality rather than quantity … and tranquil reflection rather than giddy jubilation. They weren't out to hit the front pages of the *New York Times.*

"I love this place," Jess said with all the enthusiasm you'd expect of an eager bride-to-be barely out of her teens. "It's a little bit of church heaven with a whole lot of Old West charm."

"Yes, I can't think of a better resting place for Alex … or for you and I to get hitched," Simon replied. "More than I could ever have expected, it fills me with great joy."

Jess had brought with her a box full of bluebells and forget-me-nots, symbolizing everlasting love. And she and Simon planted them around Alex's grave. Then, they bowed their heads, held each other's hands, and prayed for Alex — thanking him for inadvertently bringing them together. They held each other in a prolonged embrace and expelled their grief.

Luke told me he was impressed with the way the parks service had restored parts of the ranch to become a center for training federal workers in traditional log building.

"I have to admit I was skeptical about what they'd get up to, except a lot of partying. But I have to say they haven't done a bad job," he said. "We'd have done a much better one, though, in my day!"

"Well, we'll see about that," I said. "I have plenty of log work and legwork for you back at the lodge. I mean, why do you think I'm marrying you?"

"For my charm and good looks, presumably," he stated.

"No, for your know-how," I replied, only half-joking. I was more than ready to settle down with someone

I thoroughly trusted and with whom I could build a new life now.

Exactly a week later, Jess and Simon were married in the serene little churchyard of the rustic log chapel. Simplicity, modesty, and earthiness were the order of the day.

Jess wore a simple white silk dress with tiny flowers embroidered in lace around her neck … plus a pair of cowboy boots to add earthiness to her look.

She had a headband woven with white daisies. Her long brown hair was long and loose. She looked radiant as she held her bouquet, a dazzling mix of pale pink and white roses.

Simon was dressed in dark pants, a crisp white shirt, and a casual dark-blue linen jacket. He looked cool and classy ... and very much in love with Jess.

After the wedding vows, they exchanged identical rings, simple gold bands engraved with the word "forever." And they looked ecstatic as each slid one of the rings onto the ring finger of the other.

Priest David McNeely then pronounced them husband and wife. And they engaged in a sweet, tender kiss … one that floated around the landscape and had everyone else feeling its light but fierce intensity.

The guests shared the love and alternated between viewing the newlyweds, drinking in the fresh air and looking up at the fate-filled mountains.

I looked at Luke and said, "Something tells me they're going to make it … make it work together forever. I mean, they're made for each other."

He turned, smiled at me, and nodded in agreement.

CHAPTER 26

ONE LAST LOOK

As you can imagine, several questions still surrounded Joel's death, his mental state being chief among them. But the police found nothing untoward or particularly revelatory either in his bedroom at his father Sandy's home … or in the room he'd created for himself in my lodge barn.

But, as it was only a few days before my wedding to Luke and I wanted no unsettling surprises during our honeymoon, I thought I'd take one last look. The first thing I spotted was the stack of farrier's tools that Joel had placed in a metal container beside the shelf with the horse-grooming brushes.

My eye caught a shiny, hook-and-eye bracket he'd attached to a section of the barn's log siding. I carefully opened its latch to find a square hidey-hole that I couldn't view inside clearly because it was dark. So, I activated the torch app on my cell and shone it directly into the space, revealing a small, ornate wooden case: a keepsake box, if you like.

The blood started to rush to my head, and my hands began to shake. Wearing riding gloves, I painstakingly opened the box to find a burner phone and a notebook consisting of various scribblings, including a list of emails and phone numbers.

I immediately called Luke to tell him what I, as an untrained but inquisitive lodge owner, had discovered, and what his own professional detectives had missed. He didn't seem quite as elated as I was.

Muttering something indistinctive under his breath, Luke said he would be right over. But when he arrived on the scene like the Lone Ranger, he only stuck around long enough to scoop up Joel's belongings and to thank me perfunctorily for unearthing them.

"I think you just helped us sort out this whole damn puzzle," Luke said, seemingly more relieved than excited. "I'll have our people go over the phone with a fine-tooth comb. It'll be interesting to see what pictures it contains and what possible secrets it unearths."

The snapshots, as it turned out, were stunning in at least a couple of ways. They were of far better quality than you'd expect from a mere burner phone.

They also proved that, despite what he told sheriff's deputies, Joel had indeed been stalking Jess and Matt at the time they were arguing loudly with each other on Shadow Mountain that fateful afternoon.

The photos showed unobstructed views of curly-haired Matt as he sat slumped on the ledge from which, likely only moments later, he plunged to his untimely death.

Other pictures on the camera revealed that Joel had been far more active in tracking Simon than Luke or I had thought … at the hospital, in downtown Homage, and at the Waterview restaurant.

The mad car chase on the forest service road was clearly the culmination of a sick campaign of harassment on Joel's part. It was far from just one of those unfortunate accidents.

"He has clearly not been telling us the truth, or even a close approximation to it," Luke noted. "And I think we will find that he intentionally pushed Matt to his death, though it may be hard to prove it now that he himself is dead. I mean, he had the motive and he had Matt at his mercy."

"How so?" I asked.

"Well, after his nasty row with Jess, Matt was clearly not his usual confident, active, athletic self. He was, in fact, tired, stoned, and depressed. This would have given Joel the perfect opportunity to sneak up on him."

"But there's a big difference between opportunity and actuality," I said.

"It seems," Luke insisted, "from the pictures he took that the closer he got to Matt on that ledge the more he saw a chance to finally rid himself of his love rival.

He obviously figured he'd just give Matt a hefty shove … and let gravity do the rest. Nobody would know different."

"It's all so sad, really," I said. "Joel didn't appear to me to be a bad person, just someone who was extremely frustrated with his life and couldn't get his act together. He never learned to respect boundaries. And I blame Sandy for that."

"Blame who you want, Kyra," Luke replied. "As you know well, I'm no great fan of Sandy's. But it was Joel who was responsible for the deaths of two young men who had their whole lives ahead of them — his supposed friend Matt and himself. He's the murderous villain here, no one else."

As for Joel's diary, it was found to contain the names and numbers of local individuals "known to police" and likely involved in the drug trade and even in human trafficking. And my main thought was that Jess was well rid of him, just as I was of Sandy.

Charming, plausible-seeming people were now a red flag for me. So were angry, insecure, narcissistic bullies.

I also became convinced that the most important choice women and men can make in their lives is choosing their life partner. And it can be a hard one. As the saying goes, it's better to wait long than marry wrong.

I realized at long last that, after making at least one and possibly two disastrous choices, I was finally picking the right partner. It really was a case of third time lucky.

CHAPTER 27

WEDDING BELLS

My wedding gown was a simple, ankle-length A-line with a floaty, vintage look. It had elbow-length tulle sleeves and applique flowers in pale pink, yellow, and peach connected by light green foliage. It was stylish but understated, I thought, letting me wear the dress rather than it wearing me.

My hand-held bouquet was white baby's breath --suitably minimalist flowers that were perfect for a pragmatic, second-time bride. I put on pale leather sandals so I could walk across the grass without sinking into it and ruining my whole day.

Ali, my business tycoon friend, had helped me brush my wavy hair and loosely pin it at the back of my head, leaving wispy tendrils to frame my oval face … which a very English friend once told me was my best feature.

Ali also suggested a touch of warm pink blush on my cheeks and a daub of color on my lips. She hugged me and told me I now looked like a "sweet cherry blossom."

I thanked my lucky stars that I had a friend who knew when to take charge and when to back off and let me make my own decisions. She was a huge comfort to me.

"I like your decision to marry Luke," Ali said in a quiet, reassuring voice. "He's the right man for you. He'll let you be yourself, and he will be himself, too. And you will both be stronger together.

She added, "I wish I could find what you have."

"I know you will," I replied. "You've worked so hard all your life, and been so good to your friends. You deserve all the good things that come your way."

We had decided to hold our wedding outside in the lodge's front pasture. It was where Chelsea was helping assemble a giant display of pumpkins to welcome the annual influx of little trick-or-treaters in the fall.

We said our vows in the afternoon under a wooden archway facing Shadow Mountain. It was flanked by a semi-circle of sturdy wooden chairs well suited to the motley group of merry invitees, including newlyweds Jess and Simon, who remained radiant as roses and a prime focus of guest attention.

No one, thankfully, interrupted the proceedings when Rev. Peter Holmes asked, "Are you prepared to love and honor each other for as long as you both shall live?"

Yes, we were. Our days of doing the exact opposite were behind us. We no longer dwelled on what had gone wrong or what might have been, had we known what we know now.

We were living, and living somewhat defiantly, for today. Hitched like horses to the proverbial wagon, we'd morphed into fully fledged, rip-roaring mavericks now.

A folk band called The Bent Pennies, playing a banjo, fiddle, and acoustic guitar, provided the entertainment from the 1960s and 1970s. The youthful band members were based in Homage and were always fun, upbeat, and relatively cheap.

Their version of "The Sound of Silence" reminded everyone that "the words of the prophets are written on subway walls and tenement halls." They're also written in the mountains, the rivers, and the lodge's horse stalls.

Luke wore a light blue denim shirt that matched his Pacific-blue eyes, along with a freshly pressed pair of tan pants and the obligatory western boots.

Confident and seemingly in command, he was in the prime of life after years of unsung struggle. I was never going to be able to keep him away from me now. He had wrangled in his long-lost love, and looked pleasantly smug about it.

American journalist and author Mignon McLaughlin once said that a successful marriage required falling in love many times, "always with the same person." And looking at my cowboy cop standing tall under that archway, I could see how that might well happen.

Chef Dominique, the cook recommended for the wedding by cabbie Dale Carrick, was invariably the target of heated local opinion. Get him on a good day and he was a food wizard. On a bad one, he would leave you stewing or simmering in the lurch and never look back.

Dominique had little sense of how to mix performance and punctuality. And I held my breath as he and his crew started serving everything from complex beef and chicken dishes to sauces and salads in various diverse and unorthodox forms.

But as it turned out, I had no cause to worry. The chef, for once, had outdone himself, no doubt expecting more business at the lodge in the future.

The wedding cake consisted of sponge cupcakes with chocolate toppings that were easy to hand around, with no slicing requirements. Simple, easy, and no fuss was the way I liked it.

Some alcohol was served as valley folks love to guzzle and nibble when relaxing. And I didn't want to be known as a big killjoy on my big day. But I also wanted to provide some non-alcoholic punches to foster a layer of sobriety.

Heavily tattooed Rosy from Elspeth's Corner was one of the drinks servers. And she posted a poetic comment on her writers' website that read, "Serving drinks at a big wedding is like putting on new bedding … or watering plants in the evening, which is always so relieving."

Carrick, meanwhile, was one relieved taxi driver. In fact, he said he had never had a busier afternoon ferrying people up and down the valley. And they were never in a more giving mood. He quoted Travis Bickle in the 1976 movie *Taxi Driver* as saying "it's a long hustle, but it keeps me real busy." He added that he barely had time to toast Luke and my good fortune … and his own.

As for flowers, I had ordered bunches of them for the archway and the lodge itself from the nursery down the road. Owner Lily, herself at least twice married, was more than willing to set it all up for me. And Luke later said of the wedding: "It snowed with meat and drink … and the flowers, they were the most amazing part of it all, except for you, Kyra."

As you'd expect, the adults milled around in odd-sized groups and in clusters of raucous conversation. Boozy banker Carrie was heard telling her hunky Ken doll date that the trouble with the Homage area was that people were dull and boring. "The good thing," she added, "is that dull and boring people are often among the first to get lit."

The younger children headed for a treasure hunt (for chocolates and other candies) in the fairy hideaway that Chelsea and Jess had methodically and magically put together in the woods. The sounds of shrieking and high-pitched laughter, it seemed, echoed for miles around. Even the nearby monastery, which emphasized peace and tranquility, wasn't spared.

Everybody, in fact, was treating the wedding as an excuse to be loud and opinionated … and to generally let their hair down. Everything was on a knife edge.

Then, all of a sudden, I heard a scream from the corner of the front pasture facing the road. And I looked up to see one of the male wedding guests lying on the ground, laughing uproariously. This was followed by much hooting and hollering.

My first thought was that he'd simply had too much to drink. But I soon realized it was Rick, the out-of-work stuntman, and he'd been upended by a goat.

In fact, all my goats had escaped from their enclosure and were causing mayhem. A couple of them were even leaping on the huge rectangular haybales that we'd carefully positioned for extra seating. My thought was that goats always looked happy.

Rick's wife, Elspeth, the goat-owning cafe owner, came to the rescue in her usual no-nonsense way. She got Chelsea, Jess and Simon to act like sheepdogs and round up the prancing little devils … and gently but firmly guide them back to their paddock haven.

Everyone breathed a sigh of relief. And I was reminded of the Yiddish proverb about not approaching "a goat from the front, a horse from the back, or a fool from any side."

That was when I noticed Jacob the horse-trainer interacting playfully in the background with Appy, scratching him and repeating "there's a good boy." The pair seemed joined at the hip — just as Luke and I and Jess and Simon were now.

Ali was the keynote wedding speaker, and she sounded off eloquently about how "love still makes the world go round." She said Maverick Valley was "now on a mission to show the world that people don't need to be pushed around … at least if they stick together like our lovebirds Kyra and Luke."

I had commissioned Jacob, though, to come up with a couple of songs to round off the proceedings in a less political way. He sat gently down on a giant log by the fire that was helping warm the guests still left standing, and crooned his heart out.

I particularly liked his rendering of the famed "Song of Wyoming," based on the rugged mountain state where Jacob had once cowboyed in his youth. It spoke of just drifting and dreaming and watching the river roll by.

But it was Jacob's own original songs about the animals he loved that drew the loudest applause, particularly from the children present and especially the one about a wounded owl:

An owl flew into our deck the other night,
giving me and my wife a dreadful fright.
The northern saw-whet owl was rather small,
but it was clear it'd taken a bad fall.

My wife picked the owl up and kept it warm
to ensure there was no enduring harm.
Its feathered body and yellow eyes
were a fluffy brown bundle of great prize.

She laid it in an upturned cowboy hat
where it soon morphed into an acrobat,
swiveling around its upright head
as if it were returning from the dead.

It plumped up its body, shook its tail,
then leapt onto the balcony rail
and looked me directly in the eye
before flying off into the crimson sky.

Some say the owl is the wisest bird;
others feel it's an animal to be feared.
Certainly, it's known as a fortune forecaster
warning humans of death or disaster.

I believe owls are agents of change
in a place that's way out of our range
and rarely intersects at all with ours,
despite having superhuman powers.

I think the owl that came to us that night
may have taken a wrong turn in its flight.
It may also have wished to let us know
a little about what makes the winds blow.

I hope to meet it again some morning
when we can learn more about its warning --
and about how we humans see only a slice
of what happens in the spirit life.

Jacob also belted out a song about Blue, a maverick horse and escape artist "who never met a fence he couldn't subdue or a barrier that caused him to stew."

No, he wasn't exotic or from a zoo,
just a gentle trail horse tried and true
with plain-Jane looks, easy to misconstrue,
given he could jump like a kangaroo.

And the ranch hands never really knew
where Blue went or what was his issue.
One day, he'd stick to the pasture like glue;
the next he was off to Kalamazoo.

Horses, it was clear, would remain a big part of my family's life. And I can honestly say that, while I may live in the lodge, my home is the stable … and my heart is with Luke and the true mavericks, the mustangs of Maverick Valley. May they never be completely fenced in.

ACKNOWLEDGEMENTS

We would like to acknowledge the support of our son, Will, a professional coach who played a key role in putting together this book and is always happy to share his deep engineering knowledge and hard-earned, human-relations expertise.

Many thanks to our grandchildren, Georgia and Julian, who constantly provide us with the energy and love we need to do better for longer.

Thanks to publisher Geoff Affleck, for his unwavering professionalism, to author Nina Shoroplova for her rigorous editing, and to master illustrator Zizi Iryaspraha Subiyarta for his amazing artistic talent.

Thanks also to those who inspired this book, including close friend Dr. J. J. Milles, cousin Martin Stewart-Smith, Montana authors Tom Barrett and Glen Chamberlain, and finally, Joe Baker, Massachusetts artist, musician, and a former Wyoming cowboy.

Thanks to best friends Delia Russell, Jane Kilgour, Susy Carnaghan, Carrie Lapham, Rowan Marsh, and Jo Hoskins. And thanks again to British Columbia author

Katherine Fawcett, whose writing and writer's retreats are inspirational … and motivational.

Lastly, thanks to long-time physiotherapy partner Paige Larson for her continued friendship and collaboration over the years.

ABOUT THE AUTHORS

Rosalind Ferry is a retired physical therapist and author of four books, including one about the animals she grew up with in Africa and another about the postural problems her patients commonly faced. Her mission has always been to help patients become more self-reliant and health-conscious. But inspiration remains her love of animals and the great outdoors … and her joy in seeing people regain control over their lives by dealing with their pain.

Jon Ferry is Rosalind's horse-loving husband. He is a retired journalist who has worked for news outfits as diverse as *Reuters*, *The Globe and Mail*, and *The Vancouver Province*. He used to be a widely-traveled reporter, editor, and opinion columnist. He now writes poems about everything from trees that can communicate with each other to humans who can't. He says his best job ever was working as a horse wrangler in the mountains of northwest Wyoming.

Made in the USA
Las Vegas, NV
26 December 2025

37627157R00100